EL CUCUY

The Beginning – Part One

Alonzo Douglas

Milligan Books California

Published and Distributed by:
Milligan Books, Inc.

Cover Design:
Alonzo Douglas

Formatting:
Alpha Desktop Publishing

First Printing, September 2006
10987654321

ISBN 0-9786032-5-7

Milligan Books, Inc.
1425 W. Manchester Ave., Suite C
Los Angeles, California 90047
www.milliganbooks.com
(323) 750-3592

Table of Contents

ACKNOWLEDGMENT

Thanks to my wife, Shirley for believing in my work and my ability to create characters that will be embraced by the Latino Population and the world-at-large.

PROLOGUE

San Diego Zoo, a place where thousands of people came year-round to enjoy the matchless display of animals. Dolphins and whales dazzle the crowds of lookers-on with their acrobatic skills and an obvious show of intelligence.

Meria Rodriguez works in this lovely park. The year is 1985. She is the caretaker of the big cats. Lions, tigers, jaguar, leopards and all members of the cat family are under her supervision.

It's late Friday night. She and her son make one more round to see if all the big cats are secure. The boy comes to Cu-Rue's cage. It's a twelve hundred pound man-eater. The door is slightly ajar; the tiger is nowhere in sight. Suddenly, there's a loud noise. He looks up and sees something falling from the sky. The bright light from the object blinds him as it explodes in the air. An electric shock runs through his body as he falls helplessly to the ground.

Slightly unconscious and looking through half closed eyes, his greatest fear comes true. He sees Cu-Rue only ten feet away. Tony Rodriguez closes his eyes, leans back against the cage, and prepares to die like a man.

"EL CUCUY—THE BEGINNING"

PART ONE

Friday morning, the hospital is extremely busy. Doctors and nurses move swiftly through the corridors. A city bus carrying twenty people is broadsided downtown by a U-Haul truck driven by two teenagers, ages seventeen and nineteen.

Dr. Charleston looks on in amazement as she directs the ambulance drivers that are carrying the injured to the emergency rooms. The emergency rooms fill up quickly. Stretchers carrying the injured are being placed in the hallways under the direction of Dr. Charleston.

Only blocks away, ten San Diego police cars are in hot pursuit of the U-Haul. The U-Haul misjudges a turn and runs into a telephone pole. Without incident, the two teenagers are taken into custody.

The cops open the back door of the U-Haul, and to their surprise, it's filled to the top with mind-altering drugs in small boxes. Two words are stamped on the side of each box: Rain Forest.

CHAPTER ONE

Saturday morning, Tony Rodriguez is lying on his back in a hospital bed. A few doors down the hallway, Doctor Wong Woo sits at his desk looking at the medical report before him. He pushes the button on the intercom.

"Nurse Carlton, can you come to my office for a few minutes, please?"

The nurse answers in a very soft tone, "Yes, Dr. Woo, I'll be right there."

As she walks down the hallway to the doctor's office, she hears a strange sound. She pauses briefly as she looks around.

The doctor looks up as the door opens.

"Nurse, when you checked the patient in room A-12, what was his B.P. reading?"

"It was extremely high; it was 160 over 130."

The doctor looks puzzled. "Did you notice any facial lacerations or head wounds?"

She looks down as she thinks about the question. "Of course, Doctor, it's all right there in the chart. Dr. Martin said that the cut on his head didn't require stitches, so I treated the wound and dressed it."

Dr. Woo looks at her as if she has lost her mind.

"Doctor, is there a problem with the patient?"

"Yes, as a matter of fact, there's a serious problem." The doctor walks around to the front of the desk. He slowly picks up the chart. "Ms. Carlton, come with me, please."

"*Of course,*" says the nurse sarcastically.

The two of them leave the doctor's office and proceed down the hallway to room A-12.

"Hello, Mr. Rodriguez, how are you feeling?"

"I'm feeling just fine, Dr. Woo. And how are you, Nurse Carlton?"

They both are silent as they stare at Tony in amazement.

"You were asleep when I came on duty. How did you know my name?" asks Dr. Woo.

"I heard you and your beautiful nurse talking about my head wound just outside the door," says Tony.

"Oh, I see. Well, can you sit up for me? We're going to remove your bandage and take a look at your injury."

Tony sits up as the nurse attempts to assist him.

"How is my mother?" asks Tony.

"Your mother is doing great. She's at home, now. This might sting a little bit," says the doctor as he pulls the bandage off slowly. He turns and looks at Nurse Carlton. "As you can see, Ms. Carlton, there is no cut, so I can understand why he did not need stitches."

The young woman can't believe her eyes as she stares at Tony's forehead.

"Nurse, can you check his blood pressure while I make a phone call?"

"Yes, Doctor Woo, I'll check it again."

She moves slowly toward Tony in total disbelief.

Doctor Wong Woo enters his office. He sits down quickly, picks up the telephone and calls his assistant.

"Hello, Doctor Martin. I'm sorry to call you at such a late hour, but I have a question."

"Sure, Doctor; how can I help you?" says Doctor Martin.

"The patient that you examined in room A-12 earlier today … what was his condition upon arrival?"

The nurse walks in and hands the blood pressure results to Doctor Woo.

"Well, his blood pressure was high, and there's a nasty looking cut on his forehead. I wrote a prescription for Plendil, 10mg CR for the B.P. Is everything okay?"

"Yes, he's doing fine, except for the fact that there is no cut on his head or any sign that there ever was." Doctor Woo pauses briefly as he looks at the B.P. report. "And his B.P. is 110 over 70; his blood pressure is fine."

"I'll be there in ten minutes," says Martin.

"Oh! And another thing—he knew my name—said he heard the nurse and me talking just outside the door," says Doctor Woo.

"What's so strange about that?" asks Martin.

"Well, he heard us, and that's true. But the question is how, when we were not outside his door. We were all the way down the hall in my office with the door closed, and speaking in a normal voice tone," explains Doctor Woo.

There is silence on both ends of the phone.

Nurse Carlton is lying on the office sofa with both feet up, holding her head. All of this is too much for her.

Ten minutes later, Doctor Woo sits at his desk, reading the notes of Stan Martin, when suddenly, Stan walks into the office.

"Nurse, can you get us a blood sample from Mr. Rodriguez, please?"

"Yes, Doctor Woo. Shall I check his pressure again?"

"No, that will be all."

The two men are closely examining Tony as the nurse proceeds to draw the blood from his arm. Doctor Martin checks Tony's forehead.

"This is amazing," says Doctor Martin. He can't believe his own eyes as he feels the spot on Tony's forehead where just a few hours ago, there was a four-inch cut. Now, it's completely healed without a trace of ever being there.

Doctor Woo walks over to a small table. He picks up a small, but very sharp knife. He walks over to Tony and rubs a section of his arm with a wet cotton ball.

"What are you attempting to do?" asks Dr. Martin.

Dr. Woo remains silent as he cuts Tony slightly with the sharp knife.

Dr. Martin's response is one of surprise. "What are you doing?"

The two men watch in amazement as the open wound closes itself, and the bleeding immediately stops.

"Nurse, can you send the sample of his blood over to the lab for blood work right away, please?"

The nurse can't believe what she has just seen.

"Sure—of course, Doctor Woo."

With the sample in hand, she leaves the room.

"I believe we have stumbled upon a major medical breakthrough," says Dr. Martin with excitement in his voice.

"No one must hear of this until we know ourselves exactly what we are dealing with," Dr. Woo says, as if speaking to himself.

* * *

San Diego Zoo, midmorning, next day. Hellen Tate stands in front of Cu-Rue's cage with a microphone in hand. The news reporter puts the City of San Diego on full alert.

"Good morning, I'm Hellen Tate with KTLS news … coming to you live with the very latest report from the San Diego Zoo," says the reporter.

Lookers-on can be seen in the background as they pause and stare with curiosity at the news reporter.

She continues, "I'm standing in front of a cage—not just any cage—this particular one happens to belong to Cu-Rue, the world's largest tiger." She pauses briefly as she pulls her windblown hair from her face. "Yesterday, shortly after closing, right here in this very spot, a young man by the name of Tony Rodriguez came face-to-face with the world's largest man-eater."

The director motions for her to move in closer to the tiger's cage.

"Mr. Rodriguez barely escaped with his life. We have no knowledge at this time of the extent of his injuries."

Someone walks over and hands the reporter a sheet of paper.

"It has just been brought to my attention that the huge, twelve hundred pound killer known as Cu-Rue, has not been found. It is believed that the tiger is out there somewhere on the streets of San Diego. Please stay inside after dark until this animal is captured. The tiger has killed two men before being brought here to our zoo. Thanks for watching KTLS. I'm Hellen Tate."

* * *

San Diego Hospital, Sunday night. Doctor Woo enters the room of young Tony. The boy is standing over by the window, staring out into the night.

"Are you having trouble sleeping?" asks Doctor Woo.

Tony answers the doctor as he continues to look out the window. "No, I slept just fine today. It's the night when I want to be up and about."

Dr. Woo walks over and puts his hand on Tony's shoulder.

"How long have you had this problem?"

The boy turns and faces Dr. Woo. "Only since I've been here."

"What other changes have you noticed since you've been here?"

"Sometimes I think I'm losing my mind."

"Why is that?" asks Woo.

"I hear things that I couldn't hear before."

Tony turns toward the window again. He then turns back around quickly and looks at the doctor. "It's not just my hearing. I also see in the dark, as if it was daylight."

The doctor looks at Tony with a very puzzled look as he listens in silence.

"Even here, in my room with the door closed, I knew that you were approaching."

"Is that due to the new condition of your hearing?"

Tony pauses and smiles.

"Not only my hearing, but I can smell you—from the other end of the hall."

"Are you implying that I need a bath?"

Tony laughs loud and hard. The Doctor notices that Tony's voice has changed. It's extremely heavy.

"I don't think I should wait another minute. Come with me down to the lab. There's a few tests I must run on you right away. They might give us the answer."

* * *

12:00 midnight. It's been almost twenty-four hours since the big cat has had a meal. The smell of food draws Cu-Rue out of the darkness into the parking lot of McDonald's. There's a car at the drive-thru window. A little boy inside the car pleads with his mom to go inside.

"Mom, mom…the line is too long…please go inside."

A homeless man is standing in the parking lot with a pit bull dog on a small piece of rope, asking for money. He walks up to the lady's car as her son looks at him with curious eyes.

"Ma'am, can you please spare some change for me and my dog, Buddy? We ain't had nothin' to eat all day."

The lady rolls up her window. The little boy is watching the man as he walks away from the car. He then sees the tiger leap from the darkness. With mind-boggling speed, the dog's

14

neck is instantly broken and the big cat dashes back into the shadows with the dog in its mouth.

The homeless man screams as if he has seen the devil. He stands there, holding only the small rope that the dog was tied to just seconds before.

The little boy watched it all unfold.

"Mom! Mom! A tiger just came from nowhere and disappeared with that man's dog in his mouth!"

The little boy's mother is angry. "Haven't I told you about making up stories, son?"

The lady looks in her rear view mirror. She sees the homeless man screaming and crying.

"The man is probably losing his mind, and I don't want to hear another word."

"Mom! Please! I'm not making this up!"

The boy's mother is really angry now. "That's it, young man! You're gonna get it!"

She speeds away from the drive-thru without waiting for her change.

Back at the hospital, Doctor Woo is extremely puzzled as he looks at the results of the tests he ran.

"You look a little worried, Doc. Is anything wrong?" asks Tony.

"If I told you, you wouldn't believe it."

"At this point, I'll believe anything," says Tony.

Doctor Woo walks over to the telephone. As he begins to make his call, Tony looks at him with curiosity.

"Hello, Doctor Martin. I hate to call you so late, but I would like to meet with you here in the test lab tomorrow about noon. What I have discovered is totally scientifically unacceptable."

The doctor takes Tony back to his room.

"I'll be leaving now, but there's just a few things I need to do in my office before I go," says Dr. Woo.

"Can I let the window up?" asks Tony. "It's a little warm in here."

"Sure, go right ahead," says Dr. Woo.

Dr. Woo leaves as he closes the door gently.

Tony sits up on the side of the bed, staring at the window. Thoughts in his mind are on the big cat. He wonders if it's okay, or if the authorities have killed Cu-Rue. Maybe the cat has even taken a life. Tony wishes that Cu-Rue would come to him. He feels that he can protect the cat from the gun-happy trackers.

The ringing of the bedside phone shatters his thoughts.

"Hello?"

"Hi, Tony ... I was trying to reach Dr. Woo ... has he left already?" Tina asks.

"He said he would be in his office for a little while before he leaves. Did ya call his office?"

"Yes, I got no answer. I thought maybe he was with you."

"No; sorry I can't be of more help."

"That's okay, but there is something I'd like to talk to you about, and I know it's late, but this can't wait until tomorrow. I must see you tonight, if it's okay. I'll only stay a little while," says Tina.

Tony wonders what it is that brings her to him this late at night.

"The daylight hours is when I get most of my sleep, so you are more than welcome to come by."

He walks over to the window. He thinks to himself, if only the big cat would come to him, maybe he could get him back to the zoo without harm. Without being able to explain, he knows deep down inside that Cu-Rue is no threat to him. He also feels a special bond with the animal.

2:45 a.m. Cu-Rue walks silently through a dark alley only four blocks from the hospital. She picks up her pace as if something is driving her towards the hospital.

Tony stands staring out into the night as he thinks aloud. "Yes, that's right, come to me."

16

He stands at the window, his head is tilted back, and his eyes are closed. He can sense the movement of the big cat.

A few blocks away, Cu-Rue leaps a seven-foot fence effortlessly. A German shepherd barks as a man putting out the trash turns and catches a glimpse of the big cat as he leaps over another fence and disappears into the night.

"Help...help...please, somebody help!"

He runs toward his back door, slips and falls. Lights from nearby homes start to come on. The dog barks frantically. He breaks the chain holding him and runs in the direction of the tiger.

Tony walks over to the light switch. He turns off the lights as he looks towards the window with anticipation.

Just eight blocks from the hospital, a police officer knocks on a door in the neighborhood. The man that saw the big cat opens the door, speaking fast in a very high- pitched tone.

"Okay, sir, just calm down and tell me slowly, exactly what's going on, here," says the officer.

The man is frantically nervous as he speaks. "I was puttin' out the trash ... and I saw this huge animal jump my fence!"

"What kind of animal was it?" asks the officer.

"It looked like a grizzly bear with a long tail."

"Bears don't have long tails," says the officer.

The man continues as if he didn't hear the officer's reply. "It was black, and ... and ... and Officer, I don't know, but I do know one thing for sure ... if you don't do somethin' quick, we all gonna be eaten alive!"

The officer pulls off his hat and rubs his forehead.

"Which way did it go, sir?" the officer asks.

"I don't know, and I don't care, and YOU, Mr. Police, can go to the devil!"

The man slams the door.

The officer walks back to his car shaking his head as he wonders what he said wrong. He calls in on the patrol car radio and gives his report.

"Officer Jack to dispatch."

"This is dispatch, go ahead, Officer Jack."

"I didn't want to cause a panic out here, but I'm sure it was the tiger. I'm heading north in the direction it was last seen."

"10-4. We just received a report of a large animal laying in the street. The old lady was not sure what it was. She didn't have her glasses on. It's a block away on the corner of Vine and 10th Street. Be careful, Jack."

"10-4. I'll go check it out."

The patrol car comes to a stop. The officer gets out as he shines his flashlight on the animal. He then calls in to dispatch.

"Officer Jack to dispatch."

"Go 'head."

"There's a dead German shepherd, here. His neck is broken. Head looks like it was hit with a sledge hammer ... and his throat is ripped wide open."

Dispatch replies, "It's the big cat, all right. We'll get the tracking dogs out there while the scent is fresh."

"10-4. I'll sit here for a while, just in case it returns to the kill."

"Okay, Jack ... but keep your eyes open. This thing has tasted blood, and it's the largest tiger that anyone has ever seen, so don't take any chances."

"Don't worry, buddy, I got it under control."

"10-4, Jack. I'm over and out."

The wind is beginning to blow. There's a light chill in the air. Officer Jack removes his shotgun from the car. He checks the gun as he walks over and takes another look at the dog. Suddenly, there's a noise. Something moves behind the patrol car. The officer turns quickly with his shotgun held high. He's shaking terribly as he slowly approaches the rear of the car. The wind blows the soda can again. The officer takes a deep breath and leans back against the car. Holding his head down, he thinks out loud, "I'm too old for this sort of stuff."

He hears a low growl and slowly looks up. The man-eater has returned. The officer stares into the piercing eyes of death; twelve hundred pounds of bone-crushing terror. He can't lift up his gun. Fear has caused every muscle in his body to freeze. The tiger moves slowly towards the officer, then suddenly, with one quick motion, he leaps over the head of the police, lands on the other side of the patrol car and disappears into the darkness.

CHAPTER TWO

Back at the hospital, Tony looks at the door. He hears footsteps coming down the hall as the sweet smell of perfume fills his nostrils. A few minutes later, there's a knock on the door.

"Come in."

The door opens and Nurse Carlton enters the room. She looks around as if she expected to see someone else there.

"What brings you out at this hour?" Tony asks.

She just stands and stares.

"Well...is it that bad?"

She walks slowly toward him.

"I ran tests on your blood sample, and what I found was unbelievable, but I can't deny the facts."

She pauses briefly.

"Well...exactly what are the facts, Nurse?"

"Please, you can call me Tina. You must not tell anyone I was here, okay?"

"I'm waiting, Tina. Whenever you're ready."

She sits down beside the bed and motions for him. "Will you please sit down?"

Rain starts to fall as the wind from the sudden storm blows hard against the window curtains. Tina rushes over to close the window; she slips and falls on the wet floor. Tony goes over to assist her as the electricity goes out from the power of the storm. Suddenly, there's a flash of lightning that briefly lights up the dark room. Tony looks up. He hears something that blends in with the storm, like the sound of thunder. It's the mighty roar of Cu-Rue, the man-eater!

The nurse looks up and sees the tiger.

"Noooooooooo!" Her scream is ear shattering.

Cu-Rue is standing with her huge head in the window. She leaps inside with ease. Her eyes are glowing in the dark like two balls of fire. She's in a crouched position.

Tony thinks to himself, "No, Cu-Rue ... she's our friend."

The big cat backs away and stands still as if waiting for a command.

Tony picks Tina up and lays her gently across the bed. She has fainted. He puts his head to her chest and listens for a heart beat. After making sure she's okay, Tony turns and looks at the tiger.

"So, you can hear my thoughts?"

The big cat growls softly in acknowledgement to Tony's question.

"We must leave here tonight."

He writes a note and puts it in Tina's jacket pocket stating that fact. Tina begins to move. She opens her eyes and looks at the tiger. Tony quickly places his hand over her mouth.

"Please don't scream...she won't hurt you. We need your help." He slowly removes his hand.

Trembling, Tina speaks. "What can I do?"

"You must help us get out of here. I heard Dr. Martin suggest that I be sent to an institution."

The woman nervously watches Cu-Rue as she speaks. "I have all the answers right here in this folder. Your blood cells are going through some changes at a rapid pace. You're only nineteen...where will you go? How will you support yourself?"

"I know of a place where no one will ever find me. It's the place where I was born."

Tina looks at him in amazement.

"Where were you born, Tony?"

"It's a long story; we'll talk about it later."

"I'll take you to my place for right now. There's a small burn out back...the tiger can stay there. Quick ... get dressed ... we must hurry," Tina says.

3 a.m. A dark blue van moves through the city towards the outskirts of town. It comes to a stop at a red light. A patrol car pulls up beside the van. The police officer looks at the van, then he rolls down his window.

"Good morning, ma'am."

Tina looks over at the officer.

"Your two back tires look like they need some air. There's a station about a mile up ahead on the left hand side."

"Thanks a lot, Officer. I'll take care of it right away."

"Okay, ma'am. Be careful. There's a twelve hundred pound tiger on the loose. It's already killed twice, so you folks be careful."

The officer pulls off speedily.

Tina feels goose bumps run over her body as she drives away. Both hands are shaking on the steering wheel. She glances in the rearview mirror. The tiger's piercing eyes are on her.

"Hey, take it easy...everything's okay. Cu-Rue won't hurt you," says Tony.

The boy turns and looks into the eyes of the tiger. The big cat lies down immediately.

"See, I told her to lie down and stop looking at you because she was making you nervous."

He laughs as he sees the expression on her face.

"I didn't hear you say anything," Tina replies.

"I speak to the cat with my mind. It hears and obeys," Tony says.

"That's exactly what I want to talk to you about. These powers that you now possess ... the answers are all right here in this folder. We'll go over everything when we get to my place."

CHAPTER THREE

Los Angeles—Governor's office. Governor Turner sits at his desk looking at the pictures on the front page of the L.A. Times newspaper. He looks at the dead bodies of three young Latino teenagers that overdosed on drugs. The Governor picks up the telephone.

"Hello, Pauleen ... put me through to the mayor, please."

"Hello, Governor Turner ... one moment, please."

Pauleen pushes the intercom button. The secretary gets no response from the mayor, so she gets up and walks into his office.

"Excuse me, Mayor, but the governor is on line one."

"Tell him to call me back in five minutes. I'm talking to my wife."

The secretary goes back to her desk and picks up her phone. "Governor ... the mayor says call back in five minutes; he's on the phone with his wife."

The secretary knows the governor well. She can almost see him boiling on the other end of the phone.

"Look, Pauleen, I don't give a fat rats behind who he's talking to, you get him on the phone right now!"

She drops the phone and runs to the mayor's office, opening the door without knocking.

The mayor puts his hand over the phone before speaking to his secretary. "Pauleen, do you have a problem?"

"No, but I think you do, sir. The governor says he don't care who ya talking to. He says get your fat rats behind on the phone right now."

Pauleen turns and walks out swiftly, with a big smile on her face.

"Honey, I'll call you back. I have to answer line one; it's Turner. Okay. Bye, now."

He pushes line one and leans back in his big office chair.

"Hi, Governor Turner. What can I do for ya?"

"Don't give me that 'Hi Governor' crap. Have you read the newspaper this morning? Kids are dying in record numbers because of this drug problem that you said was under control."

"Well, Governor, I do have some good news for ya. I sent special agents in there to try and get a lead on their location. I'll hear somethin' any day, now."

"Bob, you listen to me and you listen good. You don't have the authority to send anybody anywhere. I want those men pulled out of there immediately!"

"Well, I had to send in a couple of more guys to assist Thomas Wilkes and his men, but we have not heard anything at this time, Governor Turner."

"Bob, I'm going to nail your butt to the wall on this one! I want a full report on my desk by noon tomorrow on the exact location of those men," says Governor Turner.

Many miles away, deep in the rain forest, two men stand on a makeshift lookout post. High up in the treetops on the outskirts of the camp, a temporary lab has been set up for drug manufacturing and distribution to the west and east coast. Inside of the lab, two men argue fiercely.

"Look Doc, one more slip up and your wife and daughter are going to be history!"

"I'm doing the best I can with what I have to work with," says the doctor.

Todd begins to shout at the doctor, who the drug lord brought to the rain forest to help manufacture their drugs.

"You been doing fine up until now. What went wrong? Three young boys have died this week. I've been in the drug trade for twenty years. I don't need this kind of bull!"

The doctor tries to explain. "I told Joey that the stuff was not ready to be shipped to the streets of Los Angeles. It had not been tested or cut."

"Since when did you start taking orders from Joey?"

"He said that you had talked it over with the mayor of L.A., and that the shipment was to be sent immediately."

Todd walks over to his desk drawer and pulls out a fifth of whiskey. He turns it up and takes a big swallow, as some of the liquor runs down the corner of his mouth.

"The governor is on the mayor's butt to turn up the heat on the operation. The Rowlow brothers are threatening to pull out. They are our major transporters. If we lose them, we're in trouble. Do I make myself clear?"

The light of the moon has no effect on the darkness that engulfs the rain forest, as the sounds of the night come alive. The two men standing guard are nervous.

"Hey, Dave...do you get the feeling that we're being watched?"

"Fred, I seriously believe that you have been up in this tree too long."

Something lurks in the treetops only twenty feet above the two men, and it's watching them intently.

* * *

Early morning comes with a beautiful array of colors and sounds, as the large birds spread their wings, flying from tree to tree, feeding their young.

Juvenile monkeys run rampant through the trees under the watchful eyes of their mothers.

A huge tree boa constrictor observes their seemingly reckless movement as it waits for a breakfast opportunity.

Tony walks across the back yard of Nurse Carlton's home, which leads to a huge burn. He peeps inside it. It is mid-morning. He looks up and sees the big cat up in the loft. He enters, climbs up a ladder and walks over to Cu-Rue. She lies down at his feet. He sits down beside her and rubs her gently.

Back at the governor's office, the governor walks back and forth across the office floor. There's a knock on the door.

"Come in; it's open."

The door opens, and a man with a camera around his neck is escorted into the office by two secret service men.

"Governor, this is Bill Riley. He's the mayor's nephew."

"Is that a fact? Now, exactly why are you here, Mr. Riley?"

"Well, I'm a news reporter from Shreveport, Louisiana. I heard about the problem you're having with the drug lords. I would like to cover the story, but the L.A. Times just laughed at my application."

"So, what do you want me to do? Can't your uncle help you?"

"He said his hands are tied and that maybe you could help."

Before the governor can answer the reporter, a little old man runs into the office. One of the secret service men wrestles him to the floor.

"Please ... please ... I need to speak to the governor!"

The governor is extremely angry that the man was able to get passed security.

"How the devil did he get in here?!" the governor shouts.

The two secret service men pick up the old man and start toward the door.

The old man pushes and pulls while saying, "Noooo ... no ... wait ... you must listen to me." The little man speaks with a heavy Spanish accent. "I have information about the drug lords in the jungle!"

The little man gets the governor's attention.

"Stop … let him speak."

The old man pushes the two service men away and begins to shout, "Bajate de mi miserable puercos!"

The secret service man draws back his fist, ready to take a swing.

"Bente … bente carbon!" the old man shouts.

The governor jumps up quickly from his desk and approaches the three men.

"Okay, okay … knock it off…now!"

The old man slowly turns around and walks up to the governor. They stare eye to eye for a brief moment, then, the old man speaks. "I hear that you have sent many men into the rain forest, but none have returned."

"No, I have not sent anyone to the jungle; the man who calls himself your mayor has."

The room is quiet, now. The news reporter is listening intently.

"How did you know that men have been sent there? That's top-secret information. Who are you?"

"I'm the only one who knows how to put an end to your problem. I also know that this will help you in your run for reelection."

"Okay, so you got my attention. Now tell me … exactly what do you know?"

The old man pauses, looks down at the floor, then back up at the governor.

"My name is Buscar."

The governor tries to hold back his laughter. "What kind of name is that?"

The little man smiles at the opportunity.

"It means great hunter."

"Okay, Great Hunter, now give me the information that's gonna solve my problem in the rain forest."

The governor looks at the old man as he pauses again.

"Look, I don't have all day, so say what you have to say or get out of here," says the governor.

The old man speaks slowly, "The Cucuy can rid the jungle of the drug lords. His power is far beyond normal."

One of the service men speaks out quickly, "Governor, I was born and raised in Old Mexico. My mother used to tell me that if I was bad, the Cucuy was gonna get me."

"So...then, who is this Cucuy, and where can we find him?" asks the governor.

The old man answers swiftly, "It's a Spanish word for boogie man or monster. It lives in the rain forest."

"Let me make sure I understand this clearly. So, you are telling me that a boogie man or monster is going to take care of the drug lords?" says the governor.

"I guess you could say that," the old man replies.

The governor shouts, "Then I guess you can get out of here!"

The old man tries once more to plead his case. "No, Governor, you must listen to me."

Both secret service men quickly grab the little guy by the arms and rush him outside of the governor's mansion, throwing him out onto the street. The news reporter says goodbye to the governor as he rushes out behind the three men. Buscar falls face down onto the wet street. He attempts to get up, but his ankle is twisted.

The news reporter comes over to him. As he leans down to help him, his glasses fall from his face.

"My glasses...I can't see without my glasses."

Buscar picks up the glasses and puts them on Riley's face as he's helped to his feet.

"Thanks a lot, Mr. Buscar. Let me assist you to my car ... it's just across the street."

They make their way across the street with Buscar leaning on Riley's shoulder.

Ten minutes later, they enter a small coffee shop. The cashier looks at them with curiosity as she chews her gum vigorously. They sit at the back of the coffee shop in order to speak privately.

Steam is coming from the cup of coffee as the old man drinks it, holding it with both hands.

"Hey! Don't burn your tongue; let it cool off a bit. There's more where that came from."

The attendant walks over to the table.

"Would you gentlemen like some more coffee?"

"No, I'm fine...how about you, Mr. Buscar? Would you like another cup?"

"Yes, please."

The attendant walks away, popping her gum loud and annoyingly.

"Mr. Buscar, there's a question I would like to ask you."

Mr. Buscar looks down at his coffee, then, up at the news reporter, then answers, "You would like to know if what I told the governor is true."

"Yeah, exactly. And my next question is this: how do you know it's true? Have you seen him...or whatever it is?"

The attendant returns with a hot cup of coffee. Mr. Buscar takes the coffee before she has a chance to sit it down. He takes a sip while staring at Riley, then, he speaks in a low tone, "The year was 1930. I was about twenty-five years old, working with a research crew in the rain forest."

He pauses and takes another sip of coffee.

"What were you researching?"

Buscar calmly sits his cup down, then replies, "We were in search of a very rare and elusive monkey. It is said that this monkey is over a hundred years old, and still makes babies."

"Well, how can he do that if he's really that old?" Riley asks.

"Well, word has been passed down from generation to generation that this monkey eats a plant that grows from a certain tree that has preserved his youth. Only the Cucuy knows of this plant."

31

"Tell me, Mr. Buscar … did you ever find the monkey?"

"After two months of searching, we captured the little fellow. We held him in a cage in the middle of the camp."

Buscar pauses deliberately, while taking long sips of coffee and waiting for Riley to urge him on.

"Please, please … continue Mr. Buscar."

"Three young college kids that came along with us for the research were up late one night. They were really giving it to the monkey. You know how young kids like to tease animals like monkeys."

"What were they doing to it?" asks Riley.

"They were poking it with sticks. The monkey was going crazy."

"Did you try to stop them?" asks Riley.

"I got up from my bed roll and started toward the commotion. Suddenly, I heard a sound like that of a jaguar. The three boys came running past me as if they had seen Satan."

He takes another long pause as he pushes the empty cup aside.

"Then what?" asks Riley.

"I could feel that someone was watching me. I looked up slowly and there he was, standing on a limb in a tree, only about thirty-five feet or so away from me. His eyes were like the eyes of the tiger. They were glowing in the moonlight."

The old man pauses again and waits for Riley to ask him to continue. Riley's eyes are wide with excitement.

"What happened next…did you see his face? Was it a man or beast?"

The attendant comes over and refills Mr. Buscar's coffee cup. He takes a long sip of his coffee, then looks up at Riley, causing Riley to rub his hands together with anticipation.

"The upper part of his body was kind of hidden from the moonlight. His hair was long and thick. It was not hard to tell that it was a man, and a huge one at that. He also said in Spanish, 'Leave this place.' He then made a low growl like that of a tiger."

Buscar takes another sip from his cup.

"Is that it?" asks Riley.

"Then, suddenly, with the speed of the cats, with one long leap, he lands near the monkey's cage and smashes it like it was a soda can. The monkey ran back into the jungle. The Cucuy disappeared back into the treetop."

"Did anyone else other than the three boys see him?"

"No. By the time the others got there, El Cucuy was gone. One of the boys had a heart attack. He died shortly after the encounter. The other two were so shaken up that no one could make any sense of what they were trying to say."

"Even if we found him, what makes you think he'll help? He's only one man against many men with guns. How can we win?"

Mr. Buscar smiles as he takes one last sip of his coffee before he answers.

"I cannot answer your first question, but I can answer your second one. I have heard stories that were passed down from my grandfather to my father ... there was talk of El Cucuy."

"Now wait just a cotton picking minute. I was beginning to believe you, but now I think you have drugs in your coffee. Because if what you say is true, then this Cucuy would be over one hundred fifty years old!"

Mr. Buscar looks at Riley, shakes his head, then he speaks. "You're so right, my friend. Grandfather said there's a plant somewhere in the jungle that preserves his youth."

Riley gets up, then sits back down.

"Now I know you are crazy, because if a plant like that existed, the rain forest would be flooded with people trying to find it!"

Riley stares at the old man, waiting for him to respond.

"No one believes that he exists. They all think that it's just a story that was passed down."

"Well, if what you say is really true, we must find him. But you never answered one question."

"And what question is that?" asks Mr. Buscar.

"Tell me ... how can he defeat so many people alone?"

The old man smiles before he answers, "He's not alone. It is said that he has the ability to talk to the animals with his mind, and they obey his commands. He sees in the dark as if it were day. His hearing is greater than any forest animal. He runs faster than a cheetah of Africa, and his strength is incredible."

Riley is now believing the things he is hearing.

"I think that if he only knew how many of our young Spanish kids and others are dying from the drugs coming out of the jungle, he would spring into action," says Mr. Buscar.

"Can he read and write?" asks Riley.

"I was told that his intelligence is that of a college professor," Buscar replies.

Riley then looks down at the table, then back at the old man.

"Okay ... I have a plan. I can get some of the news stories that have been released on the kids that have overdosed on the drugs, and also some pictures from my uncle's connections."

Mr. Buscar nods his head in agreement.

"There's also talk of a lady who did a study in the rain forest nineteen or twenty years ago. They say that El Cucuy is the father of her son," Buscar says.

Riley listens in amazement.

"Mr. Buscar, do you believe it's true?"

The old man just looks at Riley.

"Come on ... let's go, Mr. Buscar. We have work to do and places to go."

CHAPTER FOUR

Doctor Martin sits quietly in his home. He picks up the telephone.

"Hello, Dr. Woo ... have you heard anything on Tony or Tina?"

"No, not yet. It's been three days already," says Doctor Woo.

Have you spoken with Tony's mother?" asks Martin.

"Oh, sure. She was the first person I called. She has not heard from him. No one answers the phone at Tina's place. There's no response from her cell phone. A missing persons report has been filed on Tina and Tony, so maybe something will turn up," says Dr. Woo.

"I hope you're right. Okay, see ya."

"All right, Doctor Martin. Bye, now."

10:45 p.m. Tina drives her van down an old dirt road, forty-five miles from Los Angeles.

"What time will we be leaving for the rain forest?" asks Tony.

"Well, I have to talk to Mr. Henry, but I'm sure he'll take us there. You need to get back in touch with your mom in order to get the direct location of the cabin. Do you think it's still there?"

"I'm sure, based on what my mom said the last time we talked about it. But I'll call her once we get to Mr. Henry's place."

Tina looks at her watch.

"Well, it's almost eleven o'clock, so maybe we should call her in the morning," says Tina.

"Mom is probably 'sleep by now."

The van pulls up to a large ranch-style house. Tina blows her horn. An old man with a small dog in his arm comes out and walks slowly toward the van. Tina gets out and stretches her arms.

"Hey, Mr. Henry. How ya been, you old desert rat?" asks Tina.

The little dog jumps out of Mr. Henry's arm and runs to the back of the van, barking frantically.

Tina hugs Mr. Henry. "I've missed you since I've been working at the hospital. I hardly have time for anything anymore."

Mr. Henry looks at Tony, still sitting in the van.

"Oh, I'm sorry ... that's my friend, Tony. He needs a favor and I'm hoping you can help him."

Mr. Henry walks around to the passenger side of the van and opens the door. "Hi ya doin', young man? Any friend of Tina's is a friend of mine. You folks come on in, now; it gets chilly out here at night."

As they walk to the house, Mr. Henry turns around looking toward the van. Mr. Henry yells at the dog, "Come on, Spot! Stop barking at that van like ya crazy!"

"Oh, I forgot about our friend in the back of the van. Is it okay if she comes with us?"

Mr. Henry smiles as he answers Tony's question. "Yeah, son. Ya can't leave a lady out here all night. What kind of gentleman would do that?"

Tony walks to the back of the van. He opens the doors. The little dog comes around and looks at Cu-Rue. He turns quickly and runs past Mr. Henry and goes under an old truck sitting in the yard.

"I wonder what's gotten into that crazy dog ..." says Mr. Henry.

Tony motions for Cu-Rue to come out. The cat leaps to the ground. The van rocks as the weight of the animal is released. Mr. Henry looks at the tiger. He tries to speak, but nothing comes from his mouth.

"It's okay, Mr. Henry; she won't harm you."

* * *

Eight o'clock. Night engulfs the city of Los Angeles. Two young boys stand on the outside of a warehouse. A U-Haul truck is driven slowly up the alley toward the warehouse. One of the boys standing outside pulls out a walkie-talkie. He speaks to a boy inside the warehouse. "Hey, man, the stuff is here. They're rolling up right now."

Inside of the warehouse, twenty or thirty young boys are waiting inside to unload the truck. The big, sliding door of the warehouse is pushed back.

"Okay, let 'em in," says the boy on the inside.

"We copy; they're coming in right now," the boy outside replies.

The U-Haul comes in slowly. Before the truck can come to a complete stop, the guys are opening the doors. The lead warehouse guy starts yelling at the gang to get the truck unloaded as fast as possible.

"All right, let's get this truck unloaded; we ain't got all night! This stuff gotta be on the street by tomorrow, so move it!"

Two men are standing at the top of the warehouse stairs, looking on as the teenagers unload the truck.

"This looks like a real good shipment. This one should put us over the top," says the mayor.

"Yeah, I think you're right. The Rawlow brothers took their money off the top. They said they're going to lay low for a while until the heat is off."

"Well, Todd, I don't think we'll be needing them anymore after this one. I think I'll retire ... get out of the drug trade and move my family to a resort down in Florida."

"That sounds like a plan, Mayor."

"Todd, what about Wilkes and the other two agents?"

"Well, what about 'em?"

"I want those men released. The governor is on my butt," says the mayor.

"Well, it looks like we might have a little problem, here."

"What the devil do you mean?" asks the mayor.

Todd replies slowly, "Those agents have seen too much. They pinpointed our location despite the fact that you were supposed to have that part under control."

The mayor turns and faces Todd as he speaks. "Look, Todd, those men work for me; I hope you ain't done nothing stupid. Are they okay? And what about the two agents that were sent in to assist Mr. Wilkes?"

Todd takes a puff from his cigarette and blows the smoke out slowly.

"There's a little something called communication, Mr. Mayor."

"If anything has happened to any of those men, I'll have to work like the devil to cover it up!" shouts the mayor.

"Well, you might have to postpone your trip to Florida, Mayor. I had no way of knowing that those men were on our side."

The mayor is becoming extremely irritated at the manner in which Todd is speaking.

"Skip the b.s., and tell me what happened!"

Again, Todd speaks slow and deliberate. "It was night when they approached the lab site. Without properly identifying themselves, a gun battle broke out. Wilkes and both of his men were killed."

The mayor is a big, powerful man. He stands almost seven feet and weighs three hundred and ten pounds. He grabs Todd by the neck with both hands, lifting him off the floor and slamming him against the wall.

"Do you know who you're dealing with? I'm not one of those punks you push around in the rain forest!" the mayor shouts.

He then throws the man across the hall like a rag doll, displaying his raw strength. Todd lands on the floor, gasping for air. The warehouse guys are staring up at the two men.

"What the devil are you punks looking at? Get back to work!" shouts the mayor.

He turns back around and looks down at Todd.

"Get your sorry butt up! We have work to do."

* * *

The smell of breakfast wakes up Tina as Mr. Henry moves about in the kitchen. She walks into the kitchen, rubbing her eyes.

"Hey, looks like ya got it going on in here," Tina says.

"I've cooked a little in my day. By the way, speaking of cooking...how many chickens is it gonna take to feed that overgrown pussycat?" asks Henry.

"Only ten or twenty if she's hungry," Tina replies.

"Well, you best be on the phone with Kentucky Fried, because if she eats twenty of my chickens, I'll put a bullet in her butt."

"Now that ain't no way to treat a lady, Mr. Henry."

Mr. Henry laughs at the seriousness that is in Tina's voice.

"Okay, so maybe I won't let her have it in the rear."

"I haven't said anything to Tony about it, but I think she's pregnant," Tina says.

39

"Who's the daddy?" Mr. Henry asks laughing.

"How do I know?"

"So, ya saying she's been sleeping around?" Mr. Henry says as he laughs again.

They both are laughing as Tony enters the kitchen.

"What's so funny…did I miss something?" asks Tony.

As they finish their breakfast, Tony calls his mother. "Hi mom, how are ya? Everything is fine. No, really, I'm okay. I'm sorry I didn't call sooner. I need the location to the cabin where you did your research. No, mom, it's because I need to disappear for a while. I'll stay in touch. Please don't worry. Bye, now."

Plans are discussed and arrangements are made to receive the map from Tony's mother.

Back in Los Angeles, Buscar and Riley sit quietly as the cab driver approaches the Los Angeles airport. The two men are en route to the rain forest.

Five days later, Mr. Henry's airplane climbs high in the morning sky, as the three of them, along with the tiger, make their way towards the jungle.

It is early morning. The sun is high and the sound of the animals, birds and monkeys can be heard from the trees. Riley looks around in all directions with eyes scanning the treetops and the river's edge, as if he expects to be eaten at any moment by some ferocious creature. The Indian that is peddling the small boat through the rain forest knows the old man well. The Indian tells Mr. Buscar that he wishes to go no further. Speaking the Indian's language, Mr. Buscar asks him why.

He tells Mr. Buscar the white men are just ahead of them, carrying the power of death in their hands.

"What did he say? Why are we stopping?" asks Riley.

Mr. Buscar translates the Indian tongue to Riley.

"He's afraid of the drug lords because of their guns."

"Can you blame him?" Riley asks.

"He's gonna leave us here and come back in five moons," says Buscar.

They take their backpacks, say good-bye to the Indian, and make their way through the rain forest, cutting a small path with a machete as needed.

"I know this area of the forest well, but I didn't know that the drug lords were so close to where we have to go," says Buscar.

"Where is it that we have to go?"

"You wouldn't know if I told you. I don't know exactly where he sleeps, but I have a good idea."

"I hope you're right," says Riley, as he wipes his forehead with his bandana.

The two men are being watched as they make their way through the rain forest. Drug lords approach them from behind with guns. The two men are escorted at gunpoint to the campsite.

"It's about time you got back here. And who are these men, and why have you exposed our location?" Todd asks.

"They won't live to tell anyone," says Harry.

"Shut up, fool!" Todd shouts.

"Who are you and why are you here?"

"We are doing research of the animals on the east side of the river for a film documentary," Riley replies quickly.

"Put pops in the bamboo cage for now while we talk to the guy with the camera and see what's up," Todd says.

The reporter is beaten in attempt to get information, then, thrown in the cage with Mr. Buscar. He's half conscious as he tries to move. The old man wipes the blood from his face.

"Riley … Riley … can you hear me? Is anything broken?"

"I don't think so … just my pride."

Riley attempts to laugh at his own joke, but finds it difficult due to the pain.

Buscar looks up and catches sight of El Cucuy in mid air. He lands next to the cage, and with one effortless blow from his huge, muscular arm, the cage is shattered into pieces.

Carrying Mr. Buscar as if he weighs nothing, he quickly disappears up into the trees, leaving Riley behind.

41

Riley tries to pull a small camera from his pocket, but it all happens too fast. He lies back onto the ground, exhausted and in pain, and thinks aloud, "I must be dreaming. This can't be real."

The drug lords come running upon hearing the noise. They pick Riley up and shake him.

"Where has your friend gone? How many men was it that broke the cage open like this?" Todd points to the pieces of bamboo on the ground.

"Only one … I don't know what it was … man or beast … I couldn't tell … it moved too fast," Riley replies.

Todd hits him in the stomach and Riley falls back to the ground.

"Do you think I'm crazy?" Todd shouts.

Riley can't answer. He's holding his stomach and gasping for air.

"Pick him up and tie him to that tree over there. Don't let him out of your sight. Bill … quickly … take a couple of men and go find that old man. Hurry!"

Buscar is carried deep inside a cave, hidden by a large stone covered with a brush and a huge tree. Buscar is speechless as he looks into the cat-like eyes of a living legend … El Cucuy.

Buscar sits on the floor of the cave with his back against the wall. El Cucuy stands back in the shadows of the cave. He speaks to Buscar in a very deep voice.

"Why did you come back after so many years?"

"So you do remember me! Your memory is like the elephant," says Buscar. "Oh, Great One, our people are dying in great numbers due to the men here in the rain forest. They send the drugs to many lands; mostly the cities of Los Angeles, San Diego, but there are others," the old man says.

"What does that have to do with me, man with no name?"

"Oh! Sorry ... my name is Buscar. You look the same now as you looked many, many years ago. You have not aged ... how can that be?"

"Many men would come to the rain forest to learn the secret of youth. That secret must stay with me. Now, tell me what is it that you seek?"

Buscar walks a little closer and extends his hand out with the pictures of three young Latino boys, lying dead in the street.

El Cucuy's face is half hidden by the shadows. As he reaches out to take the pictures, Buscar notices that the hand resembles the paw of the big cat. His fingernails have grown long, taking on the look of claws. Hair has grown on the back of his hands, and thick hair covers the powerfully built arms. The hair on his head hangs down to his shoulders. His teeth slightly resemble that of the cat. His eyes glow in the shadow of the cave.

He looks at the photos briefly, and hands them back to Buscar. He lets out a low growl, then, with hands held high, he lets out a roar that can be heard for two miles or more, causing Buscar to put his hands over his ears and drop to his knees, trembling.

El Cucuy looks down at Buscar and helps him to his feet. He then speaks to him in a very deep tone with a heavy Spanish accent. "I will share my secret with you. No one else must ever know. There's a tree—deep in the belly of the jungle that blooms the flower of life. The juice from the stem of this plant is the Juice of Youth."

Buscar's eyes light up like a Las Vegas slot machine.

"I could have more money than Fort Knox with the Juice of Youth."

El Cucuy quickly grabs Buscar by the neck. "I don't find that very funny," says Cucuy.

"Please, Oh Great One! I won't tell a soul!"

"If you do, I will hunt you to the end of the earth and crush you like a fly."

"I will never betray you," says Buscar.

El Cucuy releases the old man slowly.

"Please, Oh Mighty One, tell me, how old are you?"

"El Cucuy looks at Buscar briefly before answering his question.

"I'm older than the mighty eagle that flies high in the midday sun. Older than the great turtle that feeds on the river bottom. From high in the treetops, I've watched the big cats and learned their ways, their every move, and sound. I can speak to them and they obey. My hearing is far greater. Only the eagle can match my eyesight."

Buscar is amazed. "Yes, Mighty One, I have heard of your great powers. We must free the man that came here with me. It was he who helped me to get these pictures. I know the drug lords will kill him. He's a good man," says Buscar.

"It shall be done," says El Cucuy, as he turns and walks towards the back of the cave.

CHAPTER FIVE

Tina, Henry, along with Tony and the giant cat, finally reach their destination. With map in hand, Tony leads the way to the cabin where he was born. The man that brought them from the airplane to the edge of the rain forest in his old army truck, with the back covered by canvas that hid the tiger, is still shaking as he drives back to the city.

Back at the governor's office, the governor sits at his desk. He picks up the phone and calls the mayor.

"Hello, Bob. I was told that a young fellow is being questioned by the cops on the corner of Hollywood and Vine. It was also said that this young man has information about the rain forest drug traffic."

"Okay, Governor; I'm about five minutes away, I'll get over there right now."

Inside the mayor's limousine, he and Tedy look at each other anxiously as the mayor orders the driver to go to the location. The police officer is still talking to the young man when the mayor's limousine pulls up behind the patrol car. He gets out and walks over to the officer.

"How are you doing, officer?"

"Oh, just great, Mr. Mayor. And what brings you on this side of town?"

"Well, the governor would like to speak with this young man, but if you're going to take him to the station, then maybe we'll talk to him later."

The police officer looks a little puzzled.

"Oh, no, Mayor … I'm all finished, here."

The boy willingly goes with the two men. As they ride down Hollywood Blvd., the mayor begins to question him.

"What's your name, son?"

"My name is Paul, but I haven't done anything, Mr. Mayor."

"Yeah, I know, but maybe you can help us."

The mayor pulls out a large roll of money. He gives the boy a hundred dollar bill.

"What do you know about the rain forest drug shipments?" asks the mayor.

"I know all about the operation. I have a friend who works for the drug lords, and I can help you shut them down."

"Well, we really appreciate your cooperation. How would you like to have lunch with us so we can talk more about a plan to shut them down?"

"Okay, Mr. Mayor. It's exciting to be working with you. I've only seen you on TV. I hear that you are a good man."

"Well, you heard right, son. I always try to do the right thing for people."

The mayor's cell phone rings; it's a call from the hospital.

"Hello…yes, this is he! Are you sure? I'm on my way!"

"Is everything all right, sir?" asks Tedy

"My daughter was brought to the hospital this morning … they're pumping her stomach right now. Driver, take me to the hospital in Beverly Hills and pick me up in one hour."

The driver makes a u-turn and guns the accelerator. They come to a stop in front of the emergency entrance. The mayor jumps out quickly as he shouts instructions to Tedy

"Make sure you take good care of Paul, Tedy!"

"Yes sir, Mr. Mayor. Consider it done."

The car pulls off speedily and disappears into the traffic. Tedy makes sure that the young man will not be seen or heard from again.

* * *

Shortly before nightfall, Tony finds the cabin. They go inside and can't believe their eyes. It looks the same way as Tony remembers when he was only six or seven. It's as if someone had been taking care of it. Nothing was out of place, not even a spider web.

Tony walks over to the small fireplace. He stares into the little empty space as his mind remembers some of the events that had taken place in his young childhood. He can still hear the sound of someone coming to their cabin at night as he lay sleeping near the fireplace. Too afraid to take his head from beneath the blanket, he lay still as a lamb. The sound of Tina's voice brings him back to reality.

"Hey, Tony...don't just stand there daydreaming, go get some wood and put it in that fireplace. It's a little chilly in here."

Mr. Henry looks up as he puts the backpack on the table.

"I would go, but the native women might capture me and take me to their queen," says Henry.

"Yeah, they'll take you to their queen, all right. They will put you in a pot and cook you," says Tina.

They both laugh as they see the look on Mr. Henry's face.

Tony goes out into the forest to get wood for the fire, carrying a small axe. He stops and stands still as he watches a large snake quickly ambush a monkey that was feeding on the forest floor. The coils of the big snake wrap around the monkey with amazing speed.

Other monkeys in the treetops begin to jump up and down on the branches, making loud howling noises in protest of their fallen comrade.

Tony backs away slowly, then turns to go in another direction, taking him further from the cabin. He suddenly realizes that he is lost. He turns around in a circle in order to get his bearings.

His keen sense of smell picks up a strange scent in the air. Suddenly, out of nowhere comes a huge wild boar hog with large tusks. Tony quickly runs up the tree next to him. He calls out to the big cat with his mind power, "Cu-Rue! Come to me!"

Back in the cabin, Tina and Henry wonder what is taking Tony so long. Cu-Rue gives a low growl, then leaps through the window, disappearing into the night.

Deep in the cave, El Cucuy is awakened from his sleep as he hears the cries of the boy in his mind. He lets out a deep, jaguar type growl that awakens the old man, then, with the swiftness of a jungle cat, he's gone.

The old man shakes his head and falls back asleep.

Tony looks down at the angry boar hog, which weighs about six hundred pounds. The boar walks away as if he's leaving. The small branch brakes, and Tony falls to the ground. The wild hog turns quickly, rushing toward the boy. Then, suddenly, with lightning speed, the big boar is hit from the side with the force of a Mack Truck, by a twelve hundred pound man-eater.

Teeth and claws sink deep into the flesh. The breaking of bones can be heard as the powerful jaws of the giant tiger crush the head of the wild boar, bringing instant death to the bewildered animal.

El Cucuy sits high in the treetop, observing the action. Tony can feel his presence. He looks up slowly; their eyes meet. They speak with their mental powers as to who and what they are, and how they came to be. El Cucuy gives a low growl and fades back into the forest.

Two drug dealers move through the forest in search of Buscar. El Cucuy's keen sense of hearing picks up their movement. He quickly makes his way to their location. Standing at the base of a tree, only twenty-five feet away, in plain view, the two men catch site of him.

One of them fires a shot, missing badly. With expert accuracy, El Cucuy finds his target, as the arrow from his bow sinks deep into the man's shoulder. The man's partner attempts to assist him as the giant tiger leaps from the shadows of the forest. El Cucuy orders the big cat to stop with his mind power. Tony arrives on the scene.

El Cucuy speaks to the two men as they stare at him in shock and with fear. "You must leave this place. Take your friends and your drugs with you."

The men are speechless, as the sound of his voice causes them to tremble. One of the men attempts to pick up the rifle. Tony moves with blinding speed and picks the man up by the neck, throwing him fifteen feet across the jungle floor. He then picks up the rifle and breaks it in half.

The man gets up and runs through the forest, his partner running close behind him.

Tony turns and faces El Cucuy.

"You have the strength and speed of your father," says El Cucuy in a very deep voice. "The world of mankind will never understand you and me ... we are different. We can never walk among them or live in their world. I know why you are here. You wish to escape the endless hounding of the foolish ones."

Tony listens in amazement.

"You are very wise, my father. Now I know that I can never return. But men know that we are here. We must combine our strength and drive them out of the rain forest."

They hear something coming through the brush. The three of them quickly take to the trees.

"Tony ... Tony ... where are you ... Tony ... can you hear me?" Tina yells out as she and Mr. Henry stumble through the forest.

Tony informs El Cucuy that these are his friends. Tony and Cu-Rue come down from the tree immediately.

"I'm over here!" Tony yells.

As she and Mr. Henry approach, Tony can see that the woman had great difficulty walking through the jungle. Her clothes are somewhat torn, her legs are marked and scratched.

She leans against a tree to catch her breath. Mr. Henry takes a seat on the ground. He is exhausted.

"Tony, we were worried about you. We thought that maybe you were hurt or something," says Tina, in between breaths.

"I'm okay; I got lost for a second, but I'm all right, now," says Tony.

They make their way back to the cabin.

The two drug dealers reach their campsite in terror.

"Where is the old man?" Todd shouts at the two men.

"We were attacked by a monster that fell from the trees. He shot Willie in the shoulder with his bow and arrow."

All the men in the camp begin to laugh.

"Do you expect me to believe that a boogie man jumped out of a tree and shot you with his little bow and arrow? It was probably one of the Indians that live here in the forest. Go inside and let the doctor look at your arm," says Todd.

Todd walks over to the spot where the reporter was tied up. To his surprise, there are only pieces of rope that look like they were cut with a very sharp knife. He picks up the rope and looks at it closely. He walks back over to the men.

"The guy with the camera is gone," says Todd.

"How can that be? I tied him up myself. No one could have broken that rope!" says Tom.

"Go look at where you tied him, then I want you to look at this rope and tell me what you think," Todd says with his teeth clenched.

They all walk over to the tree. Todd then gives him the rope. He rubs the edge.

"This was cut with a very sharp knife," says Tom.

"Yeah, I know that much, dummy, but who could have come in this camp with the guards on lookout?" asks Todd.

He sends one of his men to check on the lookout men. The man reports back to Todd, "They are up there on the lookout tower, all right, but they appear to be sleeping or drunk."

Todd climbs up on the lookout tower himself. First one, then the other. He climbs down and calls the men to gather around the center of the camp.

"I want every man here to keep his eyes and ears open. Those men up there were knocked out by someone."

"How could that be possible without them firing a shot? Freddy is a big man, and with the two of them up there, one should have seen something," says Tom.

"It was that thing that shot me in the arm. The Indians are afraid of our guns. They would never attack us," says Willie.

El Cucuy sits in the tree, listening to the drug dealers.

CHAPTER SIX

Back in Los Angeles, the mayor sits in the living room of his home. His wife is sitting beside him, crying on his shoulder.

The phone rings; he lets the answering machine get it. The caller leaves a message. "Hi, Mayor, this is the governor. I'm sorry to hear about the loss of your daughter. If there's anything I can do, just let me know. Please give my regards to your wife. Bye, now."

"Bob, where did we go wrong? We did the best we could. We gave her everything!" says Mary, the mayor's wife.

"That's just it, Mary, we gave her everything. We didn't give her what she really needed, and that was our time. We just didn't spend enough time with her."

Mary is crying heavily, now, as she jumps up and runs over to the bar and pours herself a drink. She turns and faces her husband and yells, "You know what killed her ... and it wasn't time that she needed from me ... yes, me, Bob! I know that you are trying to place all the blame on me! It was drugs that killed her! Drugs that you said you would protect her from. Not just any drug, it was a shipment from the rain forest! Yeah, Bob, I read the newspapers, too!"

She throws the glass of liquor at him and runs upstairs to the bedroom and slams the door.

Two days later, the governor is on the phone with the mayor.

"Bob, I got some information on the location of those drug lords today. I'm sending men in there to shut these people down. In view of what happened to your daughter, I'm sure this is music to your ears."

"When are they going in, Governor?"

"Three days from now, at midnight. We will catch them by surprise; they won't know what hit 'em."

"Okay, Governor, I'll get you a good team to go in there this time."

"No, I don't think so, Mayor. You have done enough already. Take some time off and spend some time with your wife. She will need your strength to recuperate from the loss of her daughter. Bye, now. I'll talk to you later."

The mayor hangs up. He walks over to the kitchen table quickly, and angrily turns over a chair.

It's midnight, three days later. The troops that the governor has sent to the rain forest are well prepared. Heavily armed with lethal weapons, they slowly circle the campsite. They have the camp completely surrounded. Their guns are raised and ready. The leader of the troops fires a warning shot in the air. There is no return fire or movement of any kind.

A gas grenade is thrown in one of the tents after minutes of waiting. Still, no sign of life at the campsite.

Twelve noon the next day, the governor walks back and forth across the floor in his office with cell phone in hand. He's extremely angry.

"You mean to tell me that the campsite was empty? How could that be? No one knew about it except the mayor and me. This was reliable information on their location. Are you sure that one of your men didn't mention this to anyone?!" yells the governor.

"No, sir ... absolutely not, sir," replies the lieutenant.

"I'm gonna get to the bottom of this!" yells the governor, as he slams down the phone.

Tony sits outside the cabin, staring into the jungle with Cu-Rue laying close by his side. He hears the loud snorting of Mr. Henry. He looks around as Tina comes outside.

"Tony, Mr. Henry has to be leaving in the morning, and I need to get back, also. There's enough supplies here to last you for a couple of months. By then, things will cool off and we'll come back for you."

"No ... I won't leave Cu-Rue."

"But, Tony, if you bring her back, they will kill her. She'll be safer in the forest."

"Okay, I will go to the edge of the forest with you and Mr. Henry in the morning and wait for your return."

"Are you sure you'll be all right?" asks Tina.

"Are you kidding me?" Tony replies.

They both look at Cu-Rue and laugh.

"Well, I guess that was a crazy question."

* * *

Two days have passed since Tina and Henry left. Tony thinks about her and realizes how much he really misses her. For the first time in his young life, he has fallen in love. He sees her face in his mind. The smell of her sweet perfume still lingers in his nostrils. A smile comes over his face. His thoughts are shattered when suddenly, he hears someone approaching. He orders the big cat to stay still. He opens the door.

He sees two men walking slowly towards the cabin. El Cucuy sits high in a tree nearby. Tony hears his voice mentally, saying that the two men are friends and need his help. Buscar and Riley approach Tony.

"Hi there, young man. We were told that you would help us," says Riley.

"Help you do what?" asks Tony.

"There are men that are looking for us. We need a place to hold up for a few days, and then we'll be on our way," says Riley.

"Come on in."

The two men enter the cabin, looking around curiously. They hear a low growl; they turn and catch sight of Cu-Rue standing in the corner of the room. Both men freeze with fear. The big cat walks slowly towards them. Riley faints and falls to the floor.

"Cu-Rue, they are friends," says Tony.

Buscar helps Riley to his feet without taking his eyes off the tiger.

"Please relax…she won't hurt you," says Tony.

Tony helps the old man assist Riley over to a chair by the door. Buscar takes water from his backpack, pours water on a handkerchief, and wipes Riley's face.

With his mind beginning to clear, Riley looks at the tiger; he still shakes with fear.

Tony walks over to him and puts his hand on the man's shoulder. "Please, Mr., it's all right. Trust me; Cu-Rue won't hurt you. What's ya name and why are you here? And who told you that I would help?"

The two men look at each other, then Buscar answers his question.

"My name is Buscar, and this is my friend, Riley. He's a news reporter. I met El Cucuy many years ago. The drug lords have set up a makeshift drug lab here in the rain forest. They are shipping drugs to the city of Los Angeles and other cities. Many people are dying … mostly the young. El Cucuy has agreed to force the drug lords out of the rain forest."

"You say you met him many years ago … how old were you?"

"I was doing research here in the rain forest. I was about twenty-five years old. It was El Cucuy who lead the way to this cabin."

"He says that he is my father; I believe him. But how can that be, if you met him when you were twenty-five? He looks as if he's twenty-five right now," says Tony.

"Your mother also did research in the rain forest. It was El Cucuy who came to your mother in this very cabin in the middle of the night, nineteen years ago," says Buscar.

Tony looks confused. The tiger growls as if she is in disagreement. The tiger gets the attention of Buscar and Riley.

"Tony, the reason your father looks twenty-five today, is because he is twenty-five. He stopped aging at age twenty-five."

"But how?" asks Tony.

"I will let El Cucuy tell you that. But the same blood that runs through your veins runs through his. He is your father."

Tony walks over to the fireplace and sits down on the floor as he tries to figure things out.

"You must work with your father to defeat the drug lords. It will be easy with the two of you working together."

"How did El Cucuy come to be in the rain forest?" asks Tony.

Buscar explains, "There was a plane crash many years ago, right here in the forest. His parents died on impact. It was the milk of the jaguar that kept your father alive. He was only three years old. The Missionary workers were the only ones who found him. They couldn't believe their eyes."

"What was the problem?" asks Tony.

"Well, when they found him, he was in a cave, lying with a family of jaguars; a female cat and two cubs. Normally, she would have fed the baby to her cubs. The Missionary workers followed her tracks from the plane crash to the cave, and to their surprise, they found a baby boy sucking milk along with two cubs from the mother jaguar."

"How do you know these things?" asks Tony.

"These things were told to him by the Missionary, and he told them to me."

Tony is eager to hear more.

"What happened when they found him with the cats?"

Buscar smiles, pauses briefly and waits for Tony to ask him to continue.

"Please, go on," urges Tony.

"Well, they had to shoot the mother cat in order to get the baby boy. The baby and the two cubs were taken back to the Missionary post. At the age of four or five years old, the Missionaries quickly discovered that he had the power to communicate with members of the cat family."

"Did his power come from the milk of the jaguar?" asks Tony.

"No one knows the answer, but many notes were on the plane. The Missionaries spent many hours with him, teaching him the language of his parents. They taught him how to read and write. They spoke to him in Spanish and English. Then, at the age of twenty, just before the Missionaries left, the rain forest called him, and he disappeared, only to be seen one last time by one of the Missionaries. But one year had passed. The Missionary hardly recognized him because his physical appearance had changed. It was as if the jungle had made him one of its own. And so, the legend of El Cucuy was born."

No one believes the old Missionary. Tony looks at Buscar in amazement.

CHAPTER SEVEN

The sun is going down, barely peeping over the treetops, as the drug lords move through the rain forest in search of Buscar and Riley. They come upon the cabin in the heart of the rain forest. The tiger senses their presence.

Tony also senses their movement as he motions for Buscar to be quiet and still. The drug lords ease into position. Cu-Rue jumps outside the window; Tony follows close behind the tiger. Cu-Rue goes to the right and Tony takes to the trees. The stage is set, and Buscar and Riley wait patiently.

One of the drug lords tiptoes behind the cabin with his gun held high. "Come out with your hands up!" he yells.

Cu-Rue hits the man from behind with one blow of his paw, knocking the man to the ground and unconscious. El Cucuy suddenly drops down from a tree on the other man, catching him in a headlock, which puts him to sleep immediately.

A third man stands with his rifle aimed at Cu-Rue. The tiger leaps in the air and the man fires and misses. Before he can fire another shot, the arrow from El Cucuy's bow sinks deep into the man's shoulder, causing the man to drop to his knees in pain. Tony drops from the tree, grabs the man's rifle, and breaks it in half, as if it were a twig. The three get to their feet. Tony orders the men to leave, but El Cucuy stops them.

"No, they must not be allowed to go back to their camp. They will only return with more men and more weapons. I will follow them to the edge of the rain forest. I don't think they will return."

"Take Cu-Rue with you," says Tony.

"The tiger must stay here with you in case other men are coming," says El Cucuy, as he orders the men to move. He takes the arrow from the man's shoulder with the aid of his knife. He then removes a bottle of whiskey from the man's pocket, and pours it on the wound and wraps it with leaves.

El Cucuy points towards the river. "Let's go quickly, before Cu-Rue and Ton-ka eat you alive."

The three men look up and see a huge male jaguar standing on a low tree branch. They start out in the direction of the river.

"Come on, Ton-ka," says El Cucuy.

They disappear into the forest as night finally falls. El Cucuy and the jaguar move overhead in the trees as they lead the men, while watching their every move.

Tony walks back into the cabin. Cu-Rue stays outside.

"I heard a gun shot … is everything okay?" asks Buscar.

"Yeah, everything's fine," says Tony.

Tony looks around the cabin; he notices that Riley is missing.

"Hey … where's your friend, Mr. Buscar?"

The old man looks around. The front door opens and Riley walks in looking very excited.

"Where were you?" asks Tony

"I got it all right here," says Riley.

"You got what right where?" asks Buscar.

"Pictures of the fight between El Cucuy and those men! Right here in my camera!"

"You must never show those pictures to anyone. People will come to search for El Cucuy."

"Those men that your father set free will tell everyone," Riley reasons.

"No one will believe them. Did you believe it when the story was told to you?" asks Tony.

"No … I didn't," Riley replies.

"It's for his safety and protection. He saved your life, so think about his," says Tony.

* * *

The governor stands on stage at a local college as he addresses the students in the auditorium.

"If I am reelected as the governor of the state of California, I will do everything in my power to keep educational funding at the top of my list. And the drugs that are killing so many of our young will no longer exist."

Back in the rain forest, Mr. Willie is still shaking from his confrontation with El Cucuy. He walks over to the blanket where Todd is sleeping.

"Mr. Todd, I hate to bother you, sir, but it's morning now, and our men are not back. They should have found those fellows by now, or we should have heard something."

Todd rolls over and looks up at Willie. "Yeah, you're right; they should have been back by now." Todd gets up quickly.

"Get the men up and ready; we'll be leaving for the city as soon as they're packed. I don't like the way things are going, here. I risked my life while the mayor played golf with the governor. This is it for me," Todd says.

"All right, men, let's get our things together. We're getting outta here!" Willie shouts.

One week later, Todd is on the phone with the mayor, explaining that they had to pull out because someone or something was attacking them without being seen.

"What do you mean, 'without being seen'? Are you telling me some invisible man ran you out of the rain forest?" asks the mayor.

"No … all I know is that four of our guys were hurt. Two are missing, and two of our men said they saw this thing," says Todd.

"Well, what or who was it?"

"They said it was half man and half jungle cat. I didn't see it, so I couldn't say one way or the other. But I do know that Willie saw something that scared him senseless."

"Todd, I thought the men you were working with were straight. I didn't know they were addicts. But don't worry; I'll handle it from here on out. You'll still get your cut from the money off the shipment that came in. Since the death of my daughter, I don't want anymore involvement with the drug trade."

"Mayor, I spoke to the Rawlow brothers and they want to make one more run this month, and they are gonna need your protection to help them avoid the highway check points."

"I'm out. I won't have anything to do with it. They'll have to make other arrangements."

"Mayor, you are the only one they know and trust that has direct contact with the governor."

"The answer is no."

"The Rawlow brothers can play rough, Mr. Mayor."

The mayor is outraged as he yells into the phone, "Do you think I'm afraid of some drug smuggling punks?!"

The mayor slams the phone down hard.

All is quiet in the rain forest, as Mr. Buscar and Riley say good-bye to El Cucuy and Tony.

"I'll take you to the river. I saw the Indian there this morning; he's waiting for you," says El Cucuy.

"I thank you for getting rid of the drug lords," says Buscar.

"They will return, but we will be waiting and ready. I have my son, Cu-Rue, and I have Ton-ka, as well."

"I would hate to be on the opposite side of your team," says Riley.

CHAPTER EIGHT

A few days later, Riley and Buscar are back in the city.

"Thank you, Mr. Buscar, for helping me get this story."

Riley's car comes to a stop in front of a small apartment in East L.A.

"Don't thank me; you owe everything to El Cucuy, Mr. Riley."

When Buscar gets out of the car, he leans into the window and says, "Riley, I must remind you not to show those pictures to anyone."

"I won't, don't worry. My report will say that the Indians in the rain forest shut the drug lords' operation down. It will be a good story. Only one photo shows El Cucuy. I will use the others in my report."

Mr. Buscar shakes Riley's hand. "Okay, I will talk to you later. Be careful," says Buscar.

Riley drives off with a big smile on his face. As he looks down briefly at the pictures on the seat, he puts the photo of El Cucuy in his inside jacket pocket.

A short while later, there is a knock on the mayor's door.

"Just one minute, I'm coming," says the mayor from inside. He opens the door to find Riley on the other side.

"Riley, where have you been? I've been looking all over for you. I lined up a job for you at a magazine publishing company," says the mayor.

Riley walks in and lays the photos on the coffee table.

"What's this?" the mayor asks, as he picks up the photos to examine them.

"Uncle Bob, I'm a news reporter, not some flunky for some magazine company."

"Okay, son, I get the point. Tell me, how did you get these pictures?" asks the mayor.

"I was there, Uncle Bob, with someone who knows the jungle very well. I saw the Indians attack the drug lords and drive them out of the rain forest."

"But these Indians didn't attack you and your friend?" the mayor asks.

"No, he speaks their tongue."

"What is your friend's name?"

"His name is Mr. Buscar. He is an expert tracker."

"Very good ... very good. How do you know that they were drug lords?" asks the mayor.

"The Indians know these men. They have watched them for years. Some even traded young women for drugs. Some of the drugs are in the Indian camp right now. There is enough to put these men away for life. Maybe they will tell the law who is really behind this operation once they are picked up."

The mayor looks at him curiously. "Yeah, you might be right, son. What are you going to do with these pictures?"

"You can have those. I have copies at the apartment. Well, I gotta go," Riley says, as he heads for the door.

The mayor walks with him to the door and Riley questions his uncle as to whether or not the photos will be helpful to him. His Uncle Bob assures him by telling Riley that this is the break he has been looking for to put the drug lords away.

"I'm glad to hear that, Uncle Bob. So, can you help me get the job at the L.A. Times?"

"Oh, that will be easy once I show them these photos and tell them what you went through to get them."

"That's great. Thanks a lot, Uncle Bob." Riley runs to his car.

"Keep up the good work. I'll be in touch!" yells the mayor, as Riley cranks up his car.

Riley waves and drives off.

* * *

10:00 a.m., Friday morning, Riley drives over to East L.A. and picks up Mr. Buscar. They arrive at the corner dough-nut house. Neither is aware that they are being followed. The two men following them park behind Riley's car. Riley and Buscar sit inside the doughnut house drinking a cup of coffee.

"What's the big surprise ya got for me, Riley?"

"Well, my uncle Bob, who is also the mayor of L.A., is going to get me a job at the Los Angeles Times as a news reporter."

"Hey, that's some surprise," says Buscar.

One of the men sitting in the car parked behind Riley's is on the phone.

"Hello, Mr. Mayor. We are here in front of the dough-nut house. Your nephew is inside having coffee with an old man," says Billy.

"That's good, keep an eye on them until Mark and Jerry finish searching his apartment. We must find those pictures or we'll all be in deep trouble," says the mayor.

Ten minutes later, the mayor says, "Billy, you can take off, now. Mark and Jerry found the pictures. They also found another photo in a jacket hanging on Riley's bedroom door. They said I must see it immediately, so be at my house by noon."

"All right, Mayor, we're moving out," says Billy.

The car burns rubber from the tires as it pulls away from the curb, causing Riley to look outside.

"Hey, that guy almost hit my car," says Riley.

"Probably some young kids test-driving their parents' car," Buscar says, as they both laugh.

"Well, Mr. Buscar, if it wasn't for you taking the time to take me to the rain forest, none of this would be happening for me."

"You are a smart man, Riley. You would have gotten the job done anyway."

Riley looks at his watch. "We've been here for two hours already. Time goes by quickly when you spend it with friends. That's what we always say," says Riley.

The two men tip the waiter as they head toward the door.

* * *

Five very expensive cars are parked in the long, u-shaped driveway at the mayor's house.

"I called you guys here today because we have a serious problem. Jerry, pass the pictures around," the mayor signals.

The men look at the pictures closely.

He continues, "Someone is out there making our business their business. We can check with the Indians to make sure there is no more cocaine in their possession."

"These photos can't be used against us. They prove nothing! Like you said, we can make sure that the Indians are clean," says Billy.

66

"Pass this picture around, Jerry," says the mayor.

The men look at the picture of El Cucuy and their expressions are blank.

"What in the world is that?" asks Billy.

"It's the thing that took out four of Todd's best men. They say it came into the camp and took two men that they were holding for questioning. It smashed the cage that held them and disappeared without a trace," the mayor says.

"What two men?" Mark asks.

"I don't know yet. I have to get back with Todd on that," says the mayor.

"One thing I know for sure is that we got to get rid of this thing. I'm gonna help the Rawlow brothers with one more load and then I'm out for good. Does the governor know about this half-man, half-cat that's in the rain forest?" asks Billy.

"Why should he know? This is our baby and we will put it to sleep," the mayor explains to the men.

* * *

Riley walks up the steps to his apartment. The lady that lives in the apartment next door is on her way out carrying a basket of clothes.

"Good afternoon, Ms. Neal, can I give you a hand with your basket? It looks a bit heavy."

"No, I got it, but thanks anyway."

He watches her walk across the lawn with the heavy load as she turns to face him.

"Hey! There were some men at your apartment this morning. I thought you were home because they walked right in."

"Thank you, Ms. Neal."

Riley reaches for the doorknob to his apartment, and to his surprise, the door is unlocked. He opens it slowly. As he enters cautiously, he looks all around. He notices that things are out of place. The dresser drawers are slightly open and the five hundred dollars he left on his bedside table is gone.

Riley picks up the phone and dials his uncle.

"Hi, Uncle Bob, someone broke into my apartment while I was out. They stole my rent money that I was supposed to give to the landlord today."

"I'm sorry to hear that. Was your door kicked in or a window broken?"

"No, as a matter of fact, the door was unlocked, but I'm sure I locked it when I left."

"Was anything else taken other than the money?" asks the mayor.

"Not that I can see right now."

"Well, if you need any help with the rent, just let me know."

"Okay, thanks, Uncle Bob."

The mayor hangs up the phone. He continues to address the men.

* * *

The rain forest floor is alive with activity as the animals move about. Monkeys are overhead playing a game of hide and seek. Tony walks through the forest with Cu-Rue by his side. They both feel the presence of El Cucuy, as they look up and see him in a nearby tree with Ton-ka, the huge jaguar. El Cucuy comes down.

"I have something I want to show you. Come with me."

They move through the jungle until they come to a strange looking tree.

"This is the tree of life. It cuts off the aging process," says Cucuy.

He then pulls a flower from the vine and sucks the juice from its stem. Tony takes one and does the same. He also gives Cu-Rue juice from two of the stems.

"Once the juice is in your body, you don't need to take it anymore. I take it once a month because it gives me added strength and the ability to heal immediately when I am wounded. It also makes me immune to any type of infection, even the poisonous bite of the snake."

The tiger growls and shakes her huge head. Tony looks at her.

"She's feeling the effects of the juice running through her veins," says El Cucuy.

On their way back to the west side of the jungle, Tony can feel the effect of the juice from the plant energizing his body.

"I feel strange inside," Tony moans.

"It will pass quickly. Your body is adjusting to the new change," Cucuy assures him.

"This could be a big breakthrough for the medical field," says Tony.

"It could also be the end of the rain forest. Men will come from all over the world with guns to kill other men for sole possession of the plant. No one must know of its existence," demands Cucuy.

CHAPTER NINE

Dr. Woo sits at his desk. The door opens and to his surprise, Tina enters the office.

"Tina, where have you been? I've been worried sick about you. Have you seen Tony?" the doctor asks excitedly.

"I'm sorry that I didn't call, but I was taking care of some very personal business. I hope I still have a job."

"Of course you still have a job. Now tell me, have you seen Tony?"

Tina hesitates for a moment before answering the question.

"Yes, I have seen him. Believe me when I say that he's doing fine. Just don't ask where he is, I gave him my word that I wouldn't tell."

"Tina, you must work with me. You know more than anyone the importance of this work. The possibilities are endless as to the millions of lives we could save."

"That's just it, Dr. Woo; he doesn't want to be a guinea pig!"

"Tina, I don't understand. Have you allowed yourself to get emotionally attached to Tony? You must remember that you're a medical professional. Please, let me help him understand what's happening to his body," explains Dr. Woo.

"Let me think about it for a few days and I'll get back with you. I promise," Tina assures him.

* * *

Buscar walks out of the neighborhood liquor store with a can of beer. A car pulls up beside him.

"Hey, can you tell me where Ninth Street is?"

Buscar walks over to the car. The man pulls out a gun.

"Get in and you won't get hurt," the man demands.

Buscar gets in the backseat of the car where another man is sitting with a gun pointed at him.

"We are not going to hurt you, old man, we just need some information." They blindfold Buscar. The car pulls off speedily. Shortly thereafter, they arrive at a warehouse.

"Okay, old man, get out! We just want to ask you a few questions."

They take Buscar inside and place him in a small room where they remove the blindfold.

"Sit in that chair over there. We'll be right back."

They lock the door to the room and go upstairs. They knock on the office door.

"Come in," says the mayor.

The two men enter the room.

"Mayor, we have the old man, the one who had coffee with your nephew."

"Okay, Todd, go down and take a look at him. See if he's the one you caught in the rain forest with Riley."

The door to the room opens. Buscar's eyes buck with fear as he sees and recognizes Todd. Todd looks and goes back upstairs.

"Yeah, that's the one, all right. I don't know how he did it, but he and Riley escaped my men."

"You let me worry about my nephew. I want you to find out what the old man knows about this," says the mayor, as he gives the pictures of El Cucuy to Todd.

"Frank, you and Charlie go down and see what he knows about the location of this thing in the rain forest," instructs the mayor.

Frank and Charlie both take a look at the photo and shake their heads as they both head down the stairs. The door opens and the old man stands up.

"I don't know anything, I really don't," says Buscar.

"Sit down and don't get up unless I tell you to," says Frank.

The old man sits down slowly as he looks at the two men.

"Now, tell me what you know about the thing in the rain forest that attacked you and the guy that was with you."

"No one attacked me or anyone else," Buscar says.

"So, are you telling me that this half-man, half-jungle cat is your friend?" Frank asks.

"No, I'm not saying that he's my friend, but I know he didn't attack us."

"Where in the jungle does he live?" Frank questions.

"I don't know where he lives. He didn't give me his address," says Buscar.

Charlie slaps the old man hard across the face.

"Don't be funny!" Charlie shouts.

"Please, don't! I told you all I know."

Frank goes out of the room. Minutes later, he returns with a small mattress that he lays on the floor.

"This room is where you'll stay. You are going to the rain forest with us. You are gonna show us where this thing is hiding. You will help us find him," Charlie says firmly.

"I don't think I want to find him," says Buscar.

Charlie stands Buscar up and hits him hard in the stomach. "Shut up, old man! Don't play with me, because you won't like the way I play."

"And you won't like the way El Cucuy plays," says Buscar, as he breathes heavily.

73

Charlie hits him in the stomach again and slaps him across the face. Buscar falls to the floor. Frank kicks him. Both men beat him up until he passes out.

Late in the evening, Riley drives over to Buscar's apartment. He knocks on the door.

"Mr. Buscar, it's Riley. Mr. Buscar." Riley twists the doorknob and it opens. He enters slowly and looks around. He walks into the kitchen. An untouched plate of food is on the table. The T.V. is on. Riley walks outside and looks around. He gets into his car and drives away.

* * *

Two days later, the men at the warehouse are getting ready for their trip to the rain forest.

"Make sure you double check all the weapons, men. Bring lots of ammunition. We are going to nail this thing to the first tree we get to."

The governor picks up the phone and calls the mayor. The mayor pulls his cell phone from his side.

"Hi, Governor, what can I do for you?"

"You sent me a fax stating that the drug problem was a done deal. Now, here is what I need from you—I need the names of the men that were arrested and what was found at the time of the arrest."

"Well, Governor, when my men went in there, the makeshift drug lab was destroyed. There was not a trace of any drugs. We searched the area and found no one. They have cleared out. I think they are going to try and set their operation up in the city."

"Okay, maybe you're right. I will make an announcement in my next public speech. I'll talk to you later."

The governor hangs up the phone. The mayor smiles as he orders one of the men to get Mr. Buscar ready for the trip to the rain forest.

The mayor's wife sits on the sofa in the living room of their home. She picks up the phone and calls her husband. There is no answer. She walks up the stairs and begins to run the vacuum cleaner over a floor that needs no cleaning. She notices a small cut in the carpet near the foot of the bed. Getting on her knees, she runs her hand over the cut. She pulls at the carpet and to her surprise, it folds back. Under the rug, a hole has been cut into the floor.

She sticks her hand inside and pulls out a five-pound bag of white powder. She puts it to her nose and smells it. It has no scent, but she has seen enough drug busts on the evening news to know that it is cocaine. She puts it back and lays the carpet back in its place. She falls across the bed and weeps.

"Mary, Mary, honey, I am home!" the mayor yells, as he enters the house. "Honey, where are you?"

He looks in the kitchen and then the den. He goes upstairs to find his wife lying across the bed crying.

"Mary, what's wrong?'

Mary sits up on the side of the bed and looks at her husband briefly before she answers.

"The stuff that killed our daughter is right here in our bedroom; right under our nose. She kept it in our room. How could we have been so blind?"

She yells in between tears.

The mayor walks over and helps her to her feet. He puts his arms around her as she weeps bitterly.

"No, noooo!" she yells, as she pushes her husband away from her. "Look for yourself! Look right there in the floor if you don't believe me!" she screams. "They ruled her death a heart attack, but I knew by the company she kept that she was using something. How can a young and healthy nineteen-year-old girl die from a heart attack?"

The mayor just stands there looking at her with a blank expression on his face.

"I'm going to turn this stuff over to the police. Maybe if they know the truth about her death, they'll work harder to catch the people dealing this junk!" she yells.

She runs over to the hole in the floor and drops to her knees to pull out the bag. She heads toward the door with it in hand. The mayor grabs her by the shoulders and shakes her.

"No, I can't let you do that. Think about the bad publicity it would cause. My reputation would be ruined!" he shouts, then, he snatches the bag from her quickly.

"Is that all you can think about, Bob, your precious reputation? Our daughter is dead, you stupid fool!" she yells.

The mayor slaps her hard across the face, knocking her down to the floor. He walks out of the room and slams the door shut.

Downstairs, the mayor pours himself a stiff drink. He takes a big sip then pulls out his cell phone.

"Hello, Todd, we won't be leaving tonight. There is a situation here that I have to take care of, so lay low for a few days until I give the word to move."

"All right, Mayor, we'll wait for your call."

CHAPTER TEN

Night falls over the city of Los Angeles. Buscar is lying down on a small mattress. The door to the room opens. A small Spanish boy enters with a tray of food.

"It's time to eat, Mr. Buscar," he says.

Buscar looks closely at the boy.

"Hey, are you Mr. Martinez' son? Why are you here with the drug dealers?"

"How do you know my father?" the boy asks.

"I saw you at the hospital after the accident. I'm the one that pulled your father from the car just before it exploded into flames."

"Now I remember your picture that was in the paper," says the boy.

"These men are gonna kill me if I don't help them find El Cucuy," says Buscar.

The boy looks puzzled.

"I thought El Cucuy was just a myth."

"No, son, he really exists. I'm the only one that knows how to find him. That's why I'm here."

"I heard that something half-cat, half-man attacked them in the rain forest. They also said an old man was there. So, was it you?"

The boy is extremely excited.

"Yes, son, it was me."

The boy looks at Buscar with admiration in his eyes.

"All the men are upstairs having a meeting. I will help you get out of here, but we must go quickly," the boy says.

"You are willing to risk your life for an old man?" Buscar asks.

"You saved my father's life. How can I turn my back on you? I'm not one of them. I just load and unload the trucks. I don't ask what's in the boxes," says the boy.

"They will kill you once I'm gone."

"No, Mr. Buscar, you will take me with you. They will be in their meeting for an hour or more. We can be long gone."

The boy peeps outside the door. He walks back over and helps the old man up.

"Let's go, we must hurry," says the boy.

They quickly pass the trucks as they stay low. They slide back one of the double doors just enough to peep outside. Two men are sitting outside in a car. Their heads are lying back on the headrest. They are sleeping. Once they are a few blocks away from the warehouse, Buscar uses a payphone to call Riley.

"Hello?"

"Hey, Riley, thank God you're at home. I need you to pick me up fast; I'm in trouble. There are some men after me," Buscar says urgently.

"Where are you?"

Mr. Buscar looks up at the street sign and gives Riley the location.

"I'll be right there."

"Please, hurry!"

Riley arrives ten minutes later.

"Hey, come on, let's go!" Riley yells.

They look around and see his car on the opposite side of the street. They jump in as Riley pulls off, before the door is completely closed.

"Where were you? I've been looking all over for you," Riley asks, while speeding down a dimly lit street.

"I know where I'm gonna be if you don't slow down," says Buscar.

Riley slows the car down a bit.

"Those men that attacked us in the rain forest picked me up in front of my house. They held me for a few days trying to get information on the whereabouts of El Cucuy. They were getting ready to go there to try and kill him. They have four boxes of assault rifles, according to my friend, here."

"Who is your friend?" Riley asks.

"What's your name, son?" Buscar asks.

"My name is Chico."

"He helped me escape from the warehouse," Buscar says.

"We can't go to your house, that's the first place they will look. Someone broke into my house and stole money. They also took the photo of El Cucuy, so it might be the same men. I'll take you to my Uncle Bob's house. He's the mayor, you'll be safe there until the police can get over there and nail those guys," says Riley.

Chico can't believe what he is hearing.

"No, no, Mr. Riley, you can't go there!"

Riley glances at Chico through the rear view mirror.

"Why do you say that, Chico?" Riley asks.

"I don't know how to tell you this, sir," says Chico.

"Just tell me, I'm a big boy."

"Your uncle Bob, the mayor, is the 'big boss' of the drug lords."

Riley slams on the brakes. The car spins around in the middle of the street. He then goes in the other direction to pull to the side of the road.

"What makes you think that?" asks Riley.

"I don't think it, I know it. I work there as a truck loader. The boxes in the trucks have the words 'rain forest' stamped on them. Your uncle has an office there upstairs. He's always there when loaded trucks come in."

Riley finds this hard to believe. He pulls off in the car.

"How do you know this man is my Uncle Bob? Did he tell you who he was?" Riley asks.

"No, I have seen him on T.V. I've seen his picture in the newspapers."

"Where will we go now?" Buscar asks.

"I will get you and Chico a hotel room until we can come up with a plan. I won't let Uncle Bob know that I'm on to him."

"One thing is for sure, we've got to warn El Cucuy that the drug lords are coming, so he can give them a nice, warm welcome," says Buscar.

Back at the warehouse, the men are searching for Buscar.

"I want him brought to me immediately. Find him now! Move it!" Todd shouts.

They check every inch of the warehouse. "He's not here, and Chico is missing, also," says Charlie.

"They must be together. Chico was sent down a few hours ago to feed him. I want both of them alive. Go by the old man's house and hit the streets and find Chico—now! Move it! Hurry! Don't breathe a word of this to the mayor!" Todd yells, as the men are leaving.

* * *

Two days later, Riley picks up Buscar from the hotel.

"Stay inside and off the streets, Chico, until we get back. Have your food brought up to the room. They are going to charge everything to my credit card. I've taken care of it already," says Riley.

Nervous and afraid, the boy closes the door as Riley and Buscar drive out of the parking lot.

Deep in the rain forest, El Cucuy works with Tony, helping him to sharpen his skills. He shows Tony how to make the frightening roar of the lion, tiger, jaguar and leopard, all members of the cat family. Their sound comes easy for Tony. The monkeys run for cover through the treetops. The birds take to the sky upon hearing the different sound of the big cats. Two Indian boys are trapping fish in the nearby river. After hearing the sounds, they drop their fishing nets and run.

"Here is a knife that was given to me many years ago; it is yours now," says El Cucuy.

He shows Tony how to throw the big knife with pinpoint accuracy. He cuts a circle in a tree. El Cucuy throws his knife and hits the center of the circle. At twenty feet away, Tony does the same with his knife. El Cucuy gives Tony a bow and arrow that he made for him. Tony learns quickly how to hit a target while moving through the trees.

Ton-ka, the huge jaguar, and Cu-Rue, the giant tiger, lay side-by-side on the jungle ground, watching father and son carefully.

Upon returning to the cabin, Tony lays down to rest. The big cat leaps up into a tree nearby. The sun falls fast as the night covers the forest.

Three days later, there's a knock on the door. Riley pushes it slightly; it opens. He sticks his head inside slowly and looks around.

"Hey! What's up?" says Tony, as he approaches the men from behind with a deer over his shoulder.

"Man, you scared me half to death. I didn't hear you come up," says Buscar.

"The drug lords are on their way here," says Riley.

"They're coming to get rid of El Cucuy," says Buscar.

"We will be okay, but the two of you might get hurt if there's going to be trouble, so maybe you should leave right away," says Tony.

"And miss writing a good story?" says Riley.

"Who's gonna write the story if you're dead?" asks Tony.

"I don't see any trap marks or arrow wounds on that deer. Did he just lay down for you to cut his throat?" asks Buscar.

"El Cucuy ran him down in less than a hundred yards. The takedown broke his neck, then I cut his throat to bleed it," says Tony.

The look on Riley's face is one of disbelief.

"I have heard the story that El Cucuy runs faster than the cheetah of Africa; now I know that it's not just a story," says Buscar.

Tony walks across the floor as he thinks of a plan.

"You guys will hold up at El Cucuy's cave while we deal with the drug lords. Let's get going; we don't have a moment to waste," says Tony.

"Wait, before we go, I want to give you something," says Riley.

Riley opens his backpack and pulls out a leopard colored outfit and hands it to Tony.

"This will camouflage you in the rain forest, making it not so easy for the drug lords to see you. One size fits all. At least it's close to the one your father is wearing. I made it myself."

"I was afraid of that," says Tony, as they all laugh.

"I will take the deer to the cave. We must hurry. And anyway, El Cucuy is much better at preparing the deer than I am," says Tony.

* * *

Ten o'clock Sunday morning, the mayor enters the warehouse and goes upstairs to Todd's office. He sits at the desk while constantly looking at the clock on the wall as he waits for Todd. Five minutes later, Todd walks in the room.

"Hi, Mr. Mayor, I didn't know you were coming," says Todd.

"And I didn't know that old man Buscar and Chico had left. Why didn't you call and inform me of this problem?" the mayor asks calmly.

"Well, I was hoping that the men would find them and I wouldn't have to bother you with this little matter," says Todd.

"So, you think it's a 'little matter'? You let a seventy or eighty year old man slip out of here from under your nose, and you think it's a 'little matter'? The only one that can pinpoint the location of that thing in the jungle, and you let him get away? You leave in two days—with or without him. And take some real men this time. Now, get out of my sight!" yells the mayor.

Friday morning, Todd and ten men are setting up camp in the rain forest. Their every move is being observed. El Cucuy sits high in a treetop above the men.

"Let's hurry and get set up. I want to track this thing before it gets dark. We have two of the best trackers in the world working with us. These two Indians here—Shonnee and Lyki—they know this forest like the back of their hands," says Todd.

"Can they communicate with the local Indians that live here?" asks one man.

"Of course, dummy, they lived here for twenty years," says Todd.

"Well, have they seen this thing, or can they communicate with it?" asks another man.

"This thing probably can't talk like you and me. He's been out here in the jungle, running wild. He's probably deaf and dumb. Or, maybe he grunts like a hog," says Tony, as the men all laugh.

El Cucuy and Cu-Rue sit quietly watching the men, then, suddenly, El Cucuy lets out the powerful roar of a lion. Then, he and Cu-Rue are gone like a flash.

"What was that?" one of the men asks.

"It sounded like a lion's roar," someone says.

83

"There's no lions in the rain forest; it's probably one of the cats that live here. We'll light fires tonight, and if it comes around here, it will taste some lead from a gun barrel," says Todd.

The men start out on their search through the jungle to find and destroy El Cucuy.

El Cucuy enters his cave through a trap door in the forest floor, that's covered over with dirt and leaves to conceal its existence. Upon entering the cave, he finds Riley and Buscar fast asleep. Tony is standing in the shadow of the cave, waiting and ready, with bow and arrows across his back and knife at his side. His eyes glow in the shadows like that of the jungle cat.

"Don't worry about your friends; they will be okay in here. No one can see this place from the outside unless they know where to look. But for added security, I will leave Ton-ka's brothers here. These two cats are mighty warriors. We will take Ton-ka and Cu-Rue with us," says El Cucuy.

Tony thinks about it for a minute. "Maybe if we wait until darkness, then we would have the advantage," he says.

"I think you are right. But let's keep up with their movement. I will take Ton-ka with me. You and Cu-Rue go to their campsite and remove the wooden box with the assault weapons in them. They will be left only with the guns they are carrying. I will see you back at the cave," says El Cucuy.

Todd and his men come upon Tony's cabin. They quietly surround it, as two of them approach the door with caution. El Cucuy watches in amusement from the treetop.

"Hey … you in there … come out with your hands up, and you won't get hurt!" Todd yells.

The two men standing with their backs against the wall on each side of the door wait for Todd's signal. Todd gives them the okay by waving his hand. The two men kick the door in, and with guns held high, they rush inside. Seconds later, they walk outside.

"There's no one here!" they yell.

"The rest of you wait out here—I'm going in and have a look around," says Todd.

Todd enters the cabin.

"Someone is living here, all right," says Todd. Then, he walks outside.

"Hey, John, you and four of the men will stay here. I want two inside and three surrounding the outside. You have your walkie-talkie radios, so no one should be able to get passed you without getting a bullet."

El Cucuy and Cu-Rue look down at the men as they gather around Todd to discuss their plan of attack.

"We will have three men in the trees overlooking the camp, in case he tries to attack while we sleep. The ones standing watch can get some sleep during the day. This thing is not going to be taken alive, and that's fine with me. Now, let's get back to the camp and rest. It will be dark soon. Oh! One more thing. You guys here at the cabin—try to wound him if you can, and tie him up tight. I want to get a good look at this thing before we put him out of his misery," says Todd.

The men start back to the campsite. Ten minutes later, El Cucuy returns to the cave. Riley is eating some of the deer meat that was cooked earlier. Buscar still sleeps in a corner.

"Is everything all right?" Riley asks.

"We will make our move tonight. You and Buscar must stay here. These are dangerous men with guns," El Cucuy says.

Tony enters the cave. "Not only did I remove the boxes with most of their weapons, but I managed to get one of their radios," he says.

"That's good. Now, we wait," says El Cucuy.

Night comes quickly. Tony, along with El Cucuy and the two big cats, head towards the cabin. The tips of their arrowheads have been treated with different types of toxins from the various plants in the jungle. The tips will cause a man to become temporarily paralyzed, delusional or blind, with memory loss.

Upon arriving at the cabin, they split up. El Cucuy and Ton-ka take to the trees behind the drug lords on the west side of the cabin. Tony and Cu-Rue are on the east side.

"Hey, Joe, how are things looking over there?" asks Rob.

"Everything's okay over here," says Joe.

"Benney, are you all right over there?"

"I'm trying hard to stay awake—I didn't sleep good last night," says Benney.

"Well, try and keep your eyes open, because we really don't know what we're dealing with," says Rob.

Tony stands up on a limb and makes the roar of the lion. Cu-Rue moves off to the north side of the cabin and makes a mighty roar. Ton-ka can be heard from the south side. El Cucuy can be heard making the sound of a leopard.

The men are trembling with fear as they try to communicate.

"Hey, Rob, are you okay? This is Tom, inside the cabin. We're surrounded by wild lions and tigers—you men better come in, and get Todd on the radio before we're all eaten alive."

"I hear it, but I don't know how lions and tigers can be in the rain forest!" says Rob on the radio.

"I don't know, and I don't care. But I do know I'm getting out of here," says Benney.

The moon is bright. Benney runs toward the cabin.

"No, no...come back, Benney!" Rob shouts.

Rob watches in horror as he sees a giant, black tiger leap from the darkness and without breaking its stride, picks up Benney in its powerful jaws and disappears into the night with Benney screaming.

"No...noooooooooooo!" Benney screams, and then he is heard no more.

Frozen with fear and surprise, the men can't fire a shot.

"What's going on out there? I heard someone scream!" asks Tom on his radio.

Before Rob can answer Tom's question, El Cucuy comes in through the window of the cabin.

The two men turn around. Tom screams as he feels the vice-like grip of El Cucuy's hand around his neck. El Cucuy lifts him off the ground with one hand, as he grabs the rifle with the other hand, hitting it against the wall and breaking it in half.

The other man raises his gun and shoots El Cucuy in the shoulder. Ton-ka leaps in the air, slapping the man with his huge paw. The man is out cold. El Cucuy ties the two men up tight and leaves through the window with Ton-ka close behind.

Rob hears it all on the radio. He knows it's no use in answering Tom. He tries to contact Luke on the radio.

"Luke—Luke—Answer me. Are you okay? I heard Tom scream. Is he okay?"

Rob gets no answer from either man.

Tony drops down from the treetop on Joe. To Tony's surprise, the man flips him over as they roll to the ground. The man gets up and runs. Tony hits him in the arm with an arrow that temporarily paralyzes the man. Tony picks up the walkie-talkie and answers Rob with the growl of the leopard. Rob is on his knee behind a tree. He gets up and starts to run in the direction of the campsite.

Back at the campsite, Todd picks up his radio and calls Rob.

"Come in, Rob, this is Todd. Come in, Rob ... have you seen anything? Over."

Rob pulls his radio from his side.

El Cucuy and Tony, along with the big cats, follow Rob. He runs through the rain forest, stumbling and falling, half out of his mind with fear.

"Todd, this is Rob ... come in ... over."

"Go ahead, Rob. What's going on?"

"I'm heading back to the camp. The other men are dead. They were eaten alive by wild animals," says Rob.

"What kind of animals?!" Todd shouts.

"Lions and tigers!" Rob yells.

"Are you crazy? There's no lions and tigers out here!" Todd shouts. Then, he hears the loud roar of Cu-Rue from Rob's radio.

Knocking the man to the ground, Rob rolls over as his radio and gun fall from his hand. The big cat walks toward him slowly, with fangs showing and his eyes glowing in the moonlight.

Rob screams, "Hiiiiiiiiiiiiiiii … noooooooooooooo!"

"Rob! Rob! Rob!" Todd calls out into the radio. But there is no answer.

El Cucuy drops down from the trees between Rob and Cu-Rue. He looks at Cu-Rue; the tiger stands still. He then walks over to Rob, who is lying on the forest ground, trembling.

"So, you wanted to wound me, then tie me up real tight and get a close look at me before you put me out of my misery, is that right?" he says in a deep voice.

Rob does not answer; he shakes like a leaf on a tree. Fear has locked his jaws.

El Cucuy then ties Rob up along with the rest of the men, and leaves them in the cabin.

Tony meets El Cucuy in the front of the cabin.

"We must hurry while the night is young," says El Cucuy.

They move in the direction of the drug lords' camp, along with the big cats.

* * *

Back at the campsite, Todd yells at the men.

"I want those guns now! They were here when we left. Rob and the others are dead; they were attacked and killed by wild animals. I heard with my own ears as I spoke to Rob over the radio."

"What did you hear?" asks Willie.

"I heard him scream, and I heard the roar of the tiger as it attacked him," says Todd.

"Maybe it was a wild hog; there's no tigers in the forest," Willie says.

"Fool, don't you think I have enough sense to know the difference between the roar of a tiger and the squeal of a pig?!"

Todd swings at Willie, but misses, as Willie jumps back behind one of the other men.

"Don't you ever insult my intelligence like that again!" Todd shouts.

Suddenly, one of the men looks up in a tree and catches sight of something that looks like two balls of fire. It's the eyes of the huge jaguar, glowing in the dark.

"Look! Look! Up there!" the man yells, as he points towards the big cat.

They all turn and catch sight of Ton-ka, as he growls and disappears through the darkness. One of the men fires a shot from his rifle, but hits nothing.

Immediately, they hear the roar of a lion, leopard, and the mighty roar of Cu-Rue, the tiger. The jungle comes alive with the sound of thunder. Rain begins to fall. The men panic, due to overpowering terror. They shoot up in the trees as they stumble around in confusion.

The rain clouds block out the moonlight, causing a sudden darkness to fall over the forest. With their powerful night vision, this poses no problem for El Cucuy and Tony.

Tony hits one man, then two more with arrows that cause them to be temporarily paralyzed. He hits one in the shoulder and the other in the leg. Rick hears something behind him. The drug lord turns around quickly and raises his gun. It's Cu-Rue; all twelve hundred pounds. Rick feels the sharp pain of an arrow as it hits his thigh. The poison from the tip of the arrow affects Rick immediately. He drops his gun and falls to the ground, paralyzed from the effects of the arrow.

Todd runs through the jungle. His gun is empty. El Cucuy and Ton-ka follow close behind. Tony and Cu-Rue deal with the rest of the drug lords.

Todd reaches the outskirts of the campsite. He looks for the gun box frantically.

"You lost something?" says El Cucuy.

The man turns around, surprised.

"I'm not deaf or dumb, as you can see. Maybe you are deaf and dumb ... I asked you a question," says El Cucuy.

The man is trembling. His eyes shift back and forth from El Cucuy to the big cat.

El Cucuy makes an ear-shattering roar of a lion, then leaps on Todd, knocking him to the ground.

"Hiiiiiiii!" The man screams for his life.

El Cucuy returns to the cabin with Todd. Tony is nowhere in sight. All the drug lords are tied up inside. El Cucuy drops Todd from his shoulder to the floor and ties him up. He hears the roar of Cu-Rue, as he steps outside the cabin.

"We must get out of here, fast. The National Guards with Drug Enforcement Police are coming through the forest, heading this way. One of the Indians that was with them dropped this as he ran away," says Tony.

He hands the two-pound bag of white powder to El Cucuy.

"I will leave it inside with them."

Ten minutes later, the cops arrive and surround the cabin. They take the men into custody, as El Cucuy and Tony watch from the treetops.

"I've been set up!" shouts Todd.

"You have the right to remain silent. Anything you say can and will be used against you. If you can't afford an attorney, one will be appointed to you," says the police captain.

"You better talk to the mayor, he can clear me. I don't know nothing about any drugs. This stuff was left here by a wild jungle man. Half-man and half-jungle cat!" shouts Todd.

All of the law enforcement men laugh.

"Yeah, and my father is Mickey Mouse," says the captain, as he escorts the drug lords through the forest.

"I believe the Indians attacked them, Captain, because most of them have arrow wounds," says one of the policemen.

"They sure made our job a lot easier," says the captain.

THE END

BOOK AVAILABLE THROUGH

Milligan Books, Inc.

El Cucuy $10.95

Order Form

Milligan Books, Inc.

1425 W. Manchester Ave., Suite C, Los Angeles, CA 90047

(323) 750-3592

Name_____ Date _____

Address_____

City_____ State_____ Zip Code _____

Day Telephone _____

Evening Telephone_____

Book Title_____

Number of books ordered____ Total ....$ _____

Sales Taxes (CA Add 8.25%) ....$ _____

Shipping & Handling $4.90 for one book ..$ _____

Add $1.00 for each additional book...........$ _____

Total Amount Due.....................................$ _____

☐ Check   ☐ Money Order ☐ Other Cards _____

☐ Visa   ☐ MasterCard Expiration Date _____

Credit Card No. _____

Driver License No. _____

Make check payable to Milligan Books, Inc.

_____   _____

Signature   Date